Young

Turn It Up!

• *Also by Todd Strasser* •

ANGEL DUST BLUES

FRIENDS TILL THE END

ROCK 'N' ROLL NIGHTS

WORKIN' FOR PEANUTS

Turn It Up!

A Novel by
Todd Strasser

DELACORTE PRESS/NEW YORK

Published by
Delacorte Press
1 Dag Hammarskjold Plaza
New York, N.Y. 10017

Manufactured in the United States of America
First printing

Library of Congress Cataloging in Publication Data
Strasser, Todd.
Turn it up!
Summary: Rock musicians Gary, Susan, Oscar, and Karl
are dealt a hard blow while pursuing their dream of
stardom. Sequel to Rock 'n' Roll Nights.
[1. Rock music—Fiction.   2. Musicians—Fiction]
I. Title.
PZ7.S899Tu   1984   [Fic]   83-20915
ISBN 0-385-29282-1

To Susan Pfeffer

Turn It Up!

One

It was a warm, sunny afternoon in October and Gary Specter was suffering from a serious case of puzzlement. He could have been playing basketball or back at his house practicing guitar, but instead he was searching Second Avenue for the Hole-in-the-Wall ice cream shop. He found it where an old shoe repair shop used to be. The old store had been torn down and now there was a new one with glass doors and little outdoor tables where a couple of customers sat, licking ice cream cones.

Gary pushed open one of the doors. Inside, there were more tables, a new red tile floor, and travel posters hanging on the walls. Oscar Roginoff, the keyboard player for Gary's band, was sitting at one of the tables, reading a magazine. Gary's cousin Susan sat behind a shiny display case, wearing a red-and-white-striped jacket and matching cap.

Gary walked up to the display case. "I can't believe you actually did it," he said.

"I sure did," Susan replied casually, as she nibbled on a

spoonful of chocolate-marshmallow swirl. Her wavy blond hair was pulled into a ponytail.

"But why?" Gary asked.

"Because I'm not in high school anymore and I want to see what having a full-time job is like," his cousin said.

"But what about practicing bass and rehearsing with the band?" Gary asked.

"I'll have time," Susan said. She waved her spoon around the shop. "I mean, it's no big deal. I'm just selling ice cream."

"And if we ever get signed to tour out of town or anything, you'll quit?" Gary asked.

"Ha!" Oscar laughed loudly. Gary turned and looked at him. "Tour out of town?" the keyboard player said. "We can't even get a tour around the block. Even a three-chord, no-talent bubble-gum band like the Zoomies is doing better than that."

"What are you talking about?" Gary asked.

Oscar stood up and handed Gary the magazine he'd been reading. It was a *Billboard*, the main music industry journal. "Read page forty-eight."

"Why?" Gary asked.

"Just read it and you'll see."

While Gary sat down to read, Oscar went up to the counter. He and Karl Roesch, the band's drummer, were seniors at Lenox Prep this year and he was dressed in his regulation navy blazer and gray slacks. Although he was only seventeen, the hair on the top of his head was thinning prematurely.

"How much is a free ice cream?" he asked.

"I'm not supposed to give any away," Susan told him.

"Not even to a sweet, lovable keyboard genius like me?"

Susan rolled her eyes. "Okay, Oscar, what flavor?"

"How about a sundae made with French vanilla and sprinkles and nuts and butterscotch syrup?"

Gary chuckled. "You're too much, Oscar."

The keyboard player turned to him. "Get to page forty-eight yet?"

"I'm looking." Gary flipped to page 48 and his eye caught the headline:

ZOOMIES TO TOUR

New York—The Zoomies, a Gotham-based pop band have just put the final touches on their first LP, "Zoo Time," for Phantom Records. The disc is slated for release later this month and the band will back it up with a six-week, fifteen-state tour. . . .

Gary put the magazine down. "Unbelievable."

"That's right," Oscar said. "The Zoomies, a band with less total talent than I have in my little finger. A band who we have outplayed and upstaged every time we've appeared on the same bill together. The Zoomies have produced an album and are going on tour!"

Gary rubbed his chin. This was *mucho* depressing news. His band, Gary Specter and the Coming Attractions Plus Oscar, was twice as good as the Zoomies. How could they have gotten an album contract?

Susan handed Oscar a dish of ice cream.

"You call this a sundae?" Oscar asked, staring down into the cup. "I need a magnifying glass to find it."

"Beggars shouldn't be choosy, Oscar," Susan told him. "If you don't like it, you can give it back."

But Oscar stepped back quickly from the counter and dug into the ice cream with his plastic spoon. Gary just kept staring at the *Billboard* story.

"And in the meantime, what has our band been doing?" Oscar asked. He started to count on his fingers. "Let's see. We've been playing high school dances, street fairs, and overcrowded firetraps weekend after weekend, beating our brains out and getting nowhere. I repeat, nowhere."

"If the Zoomies can get a contract, so can we," Gary said.

Oscar laughed. "Oh, really? And just how do you expect to do that? Do you think that the magic rock-and-roll fairy is going to come in the middle of the night and wave her magic wand? Do you realize that we have done nothing for the last four months except play in dumps? Sure, our fans tell us we're great. But if we're so great, how come we can't get a record contract? And how come we can't get into any of the really good clubs?"

Gary could only shrug. He'd been asking himself those same questions for weeks. What was the secret ingredient that turned a good local group into a real national act? What did they have to do to get an album contract and a video on TV? They were serious. They had original songs and an entertaining stage show. Bands with a lot less talent appeared on TV and opened for big-name acts at concerts. Look at the Zoomies. Those guys couldn't hold a tune if you handed it to them on a silver platter. Gary shook his head. You could go crazy trying to figure out why they'd gotten an album contract while the Coming Attractions hadn't.

Oscar sat down at a table on the other side of the shop, crossed his arms, and started to sulk. Gary sighed. The other thing that could drive you crazy was having a genius keyboard player who was moody and complained too much.

The door of the ice cream shop opened again and two girls came in. They were both tall and wore leg warmers and baggy sweaters. Both carried large nylon bags that were stuffed to the point of bursting.

Gary took one look and stopped thinking about Oscar. He tilted back in his chair and watched the two girls quietly. They were both very slim, wore a lot of makeup, and were really good-looking. One of them wore her hair pulled tightly back in a bun at the back of her head. The other's long auburn hair fell loosely over her shoulders. As they ordered ice creams from Susan, the girl with the long hair glanced at Gary and then looked away. But Gary's eyes stayed riveted on her. Forget good-looking. She was beautiful.

The girls paid for their cones and turned away from the counter. As they walked back toward the door, one whispered something to the other and they giggled. At the door, the girl with the long hair glanced once more toward Gary and then walked out.

Oscar usually paid no attention to girls, but as soon as they left he turned and watched through the window until they'd disappeared down the sidewalk.

"Ripton girls," Susan said, referring to a fancy girls' school nearby. "I think they take a dance class near here."

"I wouldn't mind playing at one of their dances," Oscar said.

"But, Oscar, I thought you didn't want to play high school gigs anymore," Gary said.

"I don't," the keyboard player replied. "But in their case I'd make an exception."

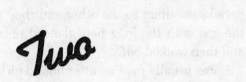

Two

Clunk! Clunk! Clunk! It sounded like someone was hitting the door with a sledgehammer. "Wake up, Mr. Rock Star!"

Gary rolled over in bed and pulled the pillow over his head.

"Oh, Mr. Rock Star, there's a call for you."

Gary opened his eyes.

"*Gary?*" his mother called.

"Okay, okay. I'm up," Gary said groggily. He turned over and looked around. His room was dim and gloomy. The window shades were drawn, but through a crack between the shade and the windowsill he could see bright daylight. The clock on the table next to his bed said 3:30.

"Should I tell them you'll call back?" his mother asked.

"No, no. I'm coming." Gary pushed some hair out of his eyes and crawled out of bed. He picked a pair of jeans off the floor and slipped them on. Still half asleep, he stumbled toward the door, trying not to step on the guitars and tape-recording equipment that was scattered about his room.

His mother was waiting out in the hall, wearing a starched, light blue dental outfit with white stockings and shoes. She must have been filling in for one of the assistants that day in Gary's father's dental office downstairs.

"Morning, Mom." Gary yawned as he passed her on his way down the hall to the kitchen.

"Morning?" Mrs. Specter said as she followed him. "I believe it is well past the time of day normal people refer to as morning. In fact, it is three thirty in the afternoon. I hope it's not too early for you."

"Very funny, Mom." Gary yawned again, walked through the kitchen, and picked the telephone receiver off the kitchen counter. "Hello?"

"I'm sorry if I got you up." It was Mrs. Roesch, the manager of the Coming Attractions and the mother of Karl, the band's drummer.

"It's okay," Gary said. "I was about to get up anyway. I don't like to sleep past four." He winked at his mother, who seated herself at the kitchen counter and poured a cup of coffee from the coffee machine. She now commenced to eavesdrop on her son's conversation. Gary pulled the phone cord as far away as it would go.

"I just wanted to tell you that I made a date for you and Karl to meet Rick Jones at Multigram Records tomorrow," Mrs. Roesch said.

"Great. What time?" Gary asked.

"Uh, I think he said four o'clock. I had it here a second ago. Can you hold on?"

"Sure." While Gary waited, he could hear the sound of shuffling paper and Karl's mother mumbling to herself.

"Here it is," Mrs. Roesch said, getting back on the phone. "A four-thirty meeting with Rick Jones. And I'll want to hear all about it on Saturday when you play the Bat Club."

"We played the Bat Club last weekend," Gary said.

"Oh, that's right," Mrs. Roesch said. "So this weekend you'll be at Razzmatazz."

"No, that's next weekend," Gary said. "This weekend we're playing at Shelter."

"Uh, of course," Mrs. Roesch said. "All right, I'll see you then." She hung up.

Gary put the phone back on the hook and shook his head. How could she survive here on earth when her brain was so deep in outer space? he wondered. Since the answer was not immediately forthcoming, he went over to the refrigerator and took out the pitcher of orange juice. He felt his mother's eyes following him.

"So that was your manager," she said from her perch at the counter. "The one who smokes pot with her son."

"Maybe she does, maybe she doesn't, Mom," Gary said as he took a glass from the shelf. "There was a time when parents thought it was cool to do stuff like that."

"Oh, certainly." Mrs. Specter laughed. "I can just see you and me sitting down some sunny afternoon on the terrace to smoke some pot together. And then perhaps we'd have some cookies and sniff a little glue."

Gary smirked and poured himself a glass of juice.

"So what did she say?" his mother asked.

Gary gulped down the juice and leaned against the sink with his arms crossed. "Would you mind explaining to me why it's so important for you to know? I mean, can't I even have a telephone conversation without having to repeat every word to you afterward?"

Mrs. Specter looked surprised. "I was just asking, Gary. Why make a big issue out of it? If you don't want to tell me, you don't have to. Of course, I'll only wonder what you're trying to hide."

You just couldn't win sometimes, Gary thought as he rubbed the last traces of sleep from his eyes. "Okay, if you really have to know, she made a date for me and Karl to go downtown and see an A and R man at a record company tomorrow."

"An A and R man?"

"It stands for artist and repertoire," Gary explained. "Basically, he's a talent scout who looks for new bands. Now, does that satisfy your curiosity?"

"Gary, I'm only curious because I'm concerned about you," his mother replied. "Most mothers do not have sons who sleep until four every afternoon."

"Sure, but most mothers don't have musicians for sons, either," Gary said. "In music you sleep during the day and work at night. It's just normal for the business."

Mrs. Specter frowned. "What business are you talking about? What work? All you do is sleep all day and play music at night. You call that work?"

Before Gary could answer, his mother went off on another tack. "And I want to know something," she said. "How did you afford all that taping equipment in your room? You're not selling drugs, are you?"

Gary sighed. His mother was convinced that practically everyone under the age of thirty was either a drug dealer or an addict. All you had to do was look a little tired or have bloodshot eyes and you were automatically suspect. At the moment, she was convinced that the mailman was a pusher and that the maid and half the assistants downstairs in his father's office were addicts.

"I know you refuse to believe this," Gary said. "But I actually make money by playing at clubs. That's how I bought that equipment."

His mother eyed him skeptically, but didn't respond. Instead she poured herself another cup of coffee. If caffeine ever became illegal, Gary thought, she'd have a $200-a-day habit, easy. Talk about addicts.

In the moment of silence that followed, he became aware of sounds coming from the dental office below. A phone was ringing and there was the high-pitched whine of the dental drill. Then someone yelled loudly in pain and the drill stopped. "Did that hurt?" he heard his father ask.

Gary poured himself a little more orange juice and faced his mother. "Look, Mom, you wanted me to finish high school and I did. But now I just want to play music. It's all I really want to do, okay?"

"But think about your future," she said. "How are you going to support a wife? How are you going to raise a family? What will they do all day while you're sleeping and all night while you're out in some club?"

Gary looked down at the floor. "I hate to tell you this, Mom. But I'm only eighteen. I'm not thinking about getting married. I mean, I don't even have a girlfriend."

"Maybe you'd have one if you spent a little less time playing rock and roll," Mrs. Specter suggested.

Gary imagined himself in a courtroom trying to explain to the jury why he'd strangled his mother with a telephone cord. *I swear, ever since I decided not to go to college she's been driving me crazy.* It was all rock and roll's fault. If he wasn't continuing his education, blame it on rock and roll. If he didn't have a girlfriend, it was because of rock and roll. He could wake up in the morning with a pimple on his nose and she'd attribute it to rock and roll.

Gary put his juice glass in the sink and the pitcher of orange juice back in the refrigerator. Then he turned to his mother and said, "I am going upstairs to practice guitar. After that I'll probably sell some drugs to the mailman so that I can take my wife and family out to dinner."

"You're not funny," Mrs. Specter said as he left the kitchen.

Three

It's not easy, Gary thought the next afternoon as he left his house to go downtown to Multigram Records, Inc. It had turned windy and colder out and Gary was wearing his old leather bomber jacket. No, it wasn't easy when people like Oscar and his mother constantly bugged him. One wanted better gigs, the other wanted no gigs at all. One wanted the rock band to be famous, the other wanted him to give it up completely. The only thing they agreed on was that, at the moment, the band was going nowhere.

Gary stopped on a corner and looked at the buildings around him, but the one he was looking for wasn't there. He started walking again.

It wasn't that the band couldn't find work. They had gigs almost every weekend. It was just that Gary had always assumed that by now they'd be recording an album and touring. He and Susan had passed up going to college for that reason. But it was October and there was still no album and no tours. There wasn't even the promise of an album.

He stopped on the next corner and looked around again. It wasn't here, either. He kept walking.

Things really were starting to get tense, he thought. This wasn't high school anymore. This was real life. Too bad there wasn't someone like a rock-and-roll guidance counselor out there who could tell them what to do in order to make it. Because he had a feeling that if something didn't happen soon, there was going to be trouble.

Gary stopped again and this time he saw a big, ugly, old-fashioned red brick building with spires and arched windows and a slanting black roof. So that was the Ripton School. He'd always known it was somewhere nearby, but he'd never bothered to find out exactly where. As he watched a group of girls come out of its big wooden doors, he found himself thinking about the pretty girl with the long auburn hair who'd come into the ice cream shop.

It would be nice to see her again. When his mother said that he might have had a girlfriend if he'd spent less time with his music, she probably didn't realize how close to the truth she was. For the last three years he'd been consumed with going to school, playing music, and keeping the band together. There just didn't seem to be time for girls. But now he was out of school, and the band had settled down into a routine of rehearsals and local gigs. Things were different.

He stood for a second more, as if hoping that the girl with the long auburn hair might appear at Ripton's doors. Then he turned toward the Lexington Avenue subway. Now that he knew where her school was, could he figure out a way to meet her? Gary looked at his watch. He'd have to worry about it later. At the moment he had a meeting to get to.

Karl was waiting for him in the lobby of the Multigram Building. He was a tall, skinny guy with a bad case of acne, and red hair that used to be long and scraggly but was now cut short. In the lobby full of business people, he looked out of place in his old green Army surplus jacket and faded patched jeans.

"Welcome to the bosom of a multinational entertainment conglomerate," he said when he saw Gary.

"Be good, Karl," Gary said. "This could be our big break."

"Oh, sure, I've heard that one before," Karl said. They started walking toward the elevator. "You brought the press kit?"

Under one arm Gary was carrying a manila envelope. Inside were some reviews of the band that had appeared in the local papers, and their self-produced single of "Rock Therapy" and "Educated Fool."

"I figured we might as well hit him with everything we have," Gary said.

"Maybe we should have brought baseball bats," Karl said. "Wouldn't that be a gas? Walk into the office with a Louisville Slugger on your shoulder and say to some honcho executive dude, 'Listen, man, sign my band to a record contract or I'm gonna bash your skull in.'"

Gary looked up at him. Sometimes Karl came up with some pretty strange ideas. "The only thing that would get you signed to would be a one-way ticket to the nuthouse."

Karl grinned and pushed the UP elevator button. "You hear about the Zoomies?"

"Oscar showed me the story," Gary said.

The silver elevator doors opened and they stepped in.

"So what did Oscar say?" Karl asked as the doors closed.

"You know," Gary said. "He wanted to be an overnight sensation yesterday."

The floor numbers lit up as the elevator rose. "He just wants to be a rock star before he loses all his hair," Karl said. "That's all the rock business is about these days. Forget the music, everyone just wants to see pretty faces up on the stage and on the TV video. You know what our band's biggest problem is?"

Gary shook his head.

"Timing," Karl said. "See, I don't want to make it big until my skin clears up. But by that time Oscar'll probably be completely bald. But if we make it now, all my zits will show up on our posters."

"That's your biggest worry?" Gary asked.

"Hey, you never had bad zits, man. You don't know what it's like."

"They airbrush those posters anyway," Gary said.

"They'll have to airbrush my whole face away," Karl said.

The elevator stopped with a lurch and Gary and Karl stepped out onto a thick red carpet. Facing them were big glass doors with "Multigram Records, Inc." emblazoned on them.

Karl took a deep breath of air, and exhaled. "Ah, smell that money!"

Gary chuckled. "Come on, let's go get an album contract." He pushed one of the glass doors and stepped into the white reception room.

In the middle of the room a young woman with frizzy brown hair sat at a desk, typing. As Gary and Karl approached she pretended not to notice them. That was no surprise. Gary knew that all the receptionists at record companies had really snotty attitudes. They had to, because all day long they were bombarded by young musicians trying to get in to see record company executives. It was the war between the hopeful rock-and-rollers and the busy company executives who couldn't be bothered with every garage band who thought they were going to be the next Rolling Stones. In that war, the receptionists were the record company's first line of defense.

Gary and Karl stopped next to the reception desk. When the frizzy-haired receptionist continued to ignore them, they started clearing their throats loudly.

"Uh-hum."

"Uh-hum-hum."

"Uh-hum-de-dum-dum."

Finally she looked up and said, "As far as I know, Multigram is not interested in frog imitations this month."

"We're here to see Rick Jones," Karl said.

The receptionist started to insert a new piece of paper in the typewriter. "Who are you?"

"Gary Specter and Karl Roesch of the Coming Attractions Plus Oscar," Gary said.

"A band of immense talent and potential," Karl added.

She laughed. "Gimme a break, guys. That's the third time I've heard that line this week." Then she looked through a calendar on her desk. "You sure you have an appointment with Mr. Jones?"

"You think we'd just come in here and pretend?" Karl asked her.

"Happens all the time, pal."

"Well, we really have one," Gary said. "Our manager made it for us."

"We'll see," the receptionist said, pointing to a row of leather couches in one corner of the room. There were already some rock-and-roll types and a couple of guys in business suits sitting there.

Gary and Karl sat down next to a guy who had long black hair and wore a blue business suit and brown cowboy boots. He was reading a copy of *Billboard* and smoking a thin cigar.

"So what else did Oscar say when he found out about the Zoomies?" Karl asked, as he settled into the couch.

"The same old stuff," Gary said. "He complained about how we're not getting anywhere. The trouble is, he's right."

"I don't see what everyone's so impatient about," Karl said. "Oscar and I aren't even out of high school yet and you and Susan just graduated last summer. I mean, it's not like we're gonna be over the hill in two months if we don't get an album contract. You said yourself that it takes some bands ten years to make it."

Gary didn't argue. Maybe he had said that it took some bands ten years. But those bands didn't have mothers and keyboard players bugging them constantly.

"The thing is," Karl was saying, "if you want to play rock and roll, you have to take some risks."

"Sure," Gary said.

"The point is to try and take intelligent risks."

This didn't come from Karl. It came from the guy in the blue suit and cowboy boots sitting next to them. Gary looked at the guy more closely. His long black hair fell over his ears like a Beatle haircut, and he was wearing aviator-style glasses that made his eyes look abnormally large. Sort of like a frog's. Gary guessed that he was in his late twenties or early thirties.

The guy smiled. "I didn't mean to interrupt, but I couldn't help overhearing," he said. "I'm Barney Star, president of Star Management." Barney reached into his suit and pulled out a shiny gold business card and handed it to Gary. It said, STAR MANAGEMENT. BORN A STAR TO MAKE A STAR.

"We already have a manager," Karl told him.

"Oh." Barney Star looked surprised. He took off his glasses and wiped them with a red bandanna he'd pulled from his pocket. His eyes suddenly looked tiny. "Sorry, man, I must have misunderstood."

"It's okay," Karl said, turning back to Gary.

But Barney wasn't finished. "Uh, you mind if I ask who he is? I know just about everyone in the business."

Karl turned back to him again. "It's my mother, actually." He sounded slightly embarrassed. No matter how good Mrs.

Roesch was or wasn't, it didn't sound very professional to say that your mother was your manager.

"Oh, I can dig that," Barney Star said, putting his glasses back on. "You want to keep it all in the family."

"Yeah, I guess," Gary said, feeling silly. He began to hand the card back to Barney.

"Hey, you can keep it," Barney said. "I got plenty of 'em. So, you played any gigs yet?"

Gary and Karl looked at each other. That was the kind of question someone would ask after finding out that a band was managed by the drummer's mother. Gary could feel his pride surge.

"We're booked every weekend," Karl said. He started naming the clubs they played at and the reviews they'd gotten. Gary could tell that he wanted Barney to understand that this was no three-chord, Top 40 baby band he was talking to.

Barney seemed to get the message. "You guys must be hot stuff. What's the name of your group?"

"Gary Specter and the Coming Attractions Plus Oscar."

Now Barney snapped his fingers. "I've heard of you. You got that real cute blond bass player and that crazy guy on keyboard."

"Yeah, Susan and Oscar," Karl said, smiling.

"You're supposed to be one of the hottest young bands in the city," Barney said, looking around the reception room. "What are you doing here?"

"Trying to get signed, what else?" Karl said.

Barney Star looked surprised. "Are you kidding? You guys shouldn't have to go through this waiting-room crap. I mean, with good management . . ." His words trailed off, as if he'd just thought of something. "Hey, listen, I don't want to take anything away from your mother, but if you ever just want to talk, or you're wondering what a *total* management company can do for you, you should give me a call, okay? I don't mind helping out and I won't ask you to sign anything in blood. Let's just say that if you're ever curious, you know where to find me."

Gary and Karl nodded and Barney stood up. "Well, look, I gotta go. One of my bands is signing a three-record deal with Arista this afternoon. It was nice meeting you dudes."

"Yeah, nice meeting you too."

Gary and Karl watched him leave through the glass doors. Then Karl turned to Gary and said, "Man, a three-record deal. I didn't even know they had three-record deals. Let me see that card, okay?"

Gary handed him the card, and Karl stared at it for a few seconds and then put it in his wallet.

"What'd you do that for?" Gary asked.

"He said if we ever have any questions we could call him, right?" Karl said. "It can't hurt."

Four

Time passes slowly when you're waiting for an A and R man. Gary looked at his watch. He and Karl had been sitting in the reception room for forty-five minutes. Gary sighed and stretched out his legs. The record company guys loved to keep you waiting. It made them feel important.

Next to him, Karl had fallen asleep.

"Ah-hum." The receptionist cleared her throat and Gary looked up.

"Mr. Jones can see you now." She pointed toward a closed door. Gary nudged Karl with his elbow.

"Whaaa?" Karl yawned.

"Time to go in," Gary said, getting to his feet.

Karl rubbed his eyes and followed.

Rick Jones's office was crammed with boxes of albums and record store displays. The walls were covered with posters of rock groups and photos of Jones with famous rock musicians. Along one wall was a fantastic-looking stereo system. At the end of the room Rick Jones himself sat behind a desk cluttered with papers, reels of recording tape, and video cassettes. Gary thought he looked pretty young. He had long straight blond hair and was wearing a western-style shirt and jeans. Gary had heard that most A and R guys secretly wished they were rock stars. Jones sure looked like he did.

The A and R man was on the phone. Actually, he was on two phones at once, holding a black phone to one ear and a red phone to the other. When he saw Gary and Karl, he pointed at two chairs and continued with his conversations. Gary and Karl sat down.

"Yeah, I know he said he'd have the master mixed last week," Jones said into the red phone. "But it isn't finished. What? Okay, I'll tell him." He turned to the black phone. "He says if you don't have that master mixed by Wednesday he's gonna cancel your tour. What? Okay, I'll tell him." Jones turned back to the red phone. "He says if you cancel the tour he'll sue the crap out of you. What? Okay, I'll tell him. . . ."

Gary and Karl watched as Jones went back and forth between the two phones. He even managed to stick a cigarette between his lips and light it.

A few minutes later the telephone conversation ended with everyone threatening to sue the crap out of each other. Rick Jones hung up both phones, rubbed his forehead wearily, and looked at Gary and Karl.

"Who are you?" he asked.

"I'm Gary Specter of Gary Specter and the Coming Attractions Plus Oscar and this is Karl, our drummer," Gary explained.

"The Coming Attractions," Jones mumbled, and started to rummage through a pile of loose papers and notes on his desk. "A local band, right? I spoke to a lady named Roesch. What is she, your manager?"

Karl nodded.

"How come I never heard of her before?" Jones asked. "Does she manage any other bands?"

"Well, uh, no," Karl said. "Actually, she's my mother."

"Your mother?" Jones gave Karl and Gary a funny look, then leaned back in his chair and took a drag off his cigarette. The A and R man blew a smoke ring toward the ceiling. "Okay, I don't have a lot of time," he said. "What do you want?"

"Could you come to our gig at Shelter this weekend and see us perform?" Karl asked.

Rick Jones looked amused. "I don't know. Why should I?"

Gary could tell by his tone that he didn't take them seriously. Still, they had to try. "Because we're good and we have more than enough material for an album," he said. "All we need is a chance."

"And we put on a great live show," Karl added.

Rick Jones chuckled and looked more closely at Karl. "You know how many times a week I hear that?" he asked. "If you're so great, how come you're playing in a dump like Shelter?"

Neither Gary nor Karl had a quick answer. Jones pointed at the envelope Gary was holding. "What have you got there?"

"Our press kit and demo record," Gary said, pushing the envelope across the desk.

Jones glanced in the envelope for a few seconds and skimmed a couple of reviews. He picked out the band's single. "You record this yourself?"

"Yeah," Karl said. "It got a lot of play on WHAT last year. And Bleecker Joe did a whole window display on it."

"Maybe you could listen to it," Gary said.

"Not right now." Jones tossed the record on top of a pile of singles and tapes and video cassettes on his desk. Then he leaned toward Gary and Karl. "Listen," he said. "There are a million bands that want me to come see them. I could grow old before I heard every band that comes in here."

"But we're really good," Karl said. "We write original songs that people really like and we put on a good show. We've already got a following here in the city. Clubs ask us to play all the time."

Rick Jones shrugged. "What can I tell you? There was a time once in this business when a couple of young kids like you could have walked into this place with those reviews and that demo and someone probably would have given you a chance. Maybe they would have put you in a studio with a producer for a week, just to see what you'd come up with. But those days are over. The public doesn't buy records the way they used to. The whole industry is different. No one's throwing money around anymore. You want to know how many new acts I signed last year? Seven. Seven new acts for the whole year! I'm not even sure *I know* what you have to do to make it as a rock band anymore. All I know is that today you have to be more than good. You have to be special."

"My mother says I'm special," Karl said.

Gary groaned.

But Rick Jones smiled. "Yeah, I know. My mother said the same thing about me and now I'm an A and R man." Then he pushed the manila envelope back across the desk to Gary. "Look, I can give you one hint. You're not gonna get discovered playing in places like Shelter. If you want to make it, you're gonna have to get into the big clubs like the Bottom Line and DeLux. Especially DeLux. They've been using a lot of new bands for their opening acts on weekday nights. It's really good exposure."

"Our manager has been trying for months to get us in there," Gary said. "But they just don't seem interested."

Jones nodded. "No offense or anything, but my mother probably couldn't get me in there, either. Most bands have professional management companies fronting them. It's just one of the facts of life in this business. Women's lib still hasn't made it to rock and roll."

With that, the A and R man stood up and thanked Gary and Karl for coming. The next thing they knew, they were walking back through the reception area and out the glass doors.

"So what do you think?" Karl asked.

Gary shook his head slowly. "At least he was honest."

Five

A few nights later Gary watched Oscar pace around the dressing room at Shelter. The room was like a prison cell. Old gray paint was peeling off the walls and a single bare light bulb hung from the ceiling. A cold, wet draft came through a cracked window, making the band shiver while they waited for their cue to go on.

"Don't you just love the decor?" Oscar asked as he walked around the room in the formal coat and tails he always wore for shows. "I can't decide whether it reminds me more of Early American cockroach or Greco-European garbage can."

He stopped before Karl, who was sitting on an old green couch with split seams and brown stuffing leaking out of it. The drummer was smoking his customary pregig joint.

"How can you even sit on that thing?" Oscar asked him. "It looks like something might crawl out of it at any second."

Karl took a deep toke off the joint and started to cough. "I've been vaccinated," he wheezed.

Oscar snorted and walked away. "What are we doing here?" he asked. "Why are we waiting to play in this rat's nest? What do we hope to gain by this wonderful experience?"

No one answered. Oscar stopped next to Susan, who had picked up a broken mirror from the floor and set it on the windowsill. She was wearing a tight, low-cut green dress, orange fishnet stockings, and green high heels. Around her eyes she'd put on black eyeliner and glittery green eye shadow.

"Oh, Oscar," she said, turning sideways to the mirror and pulling the dress tightly against her stomach. "I've only been working in that stupid ice cream shop for a week and already this dress feels tight on me. See? I've suddenly got a little tummy."

"You sure it's from ice cream?" Karl asked from across the room.

Susan shot him a dirty look. "I *know* it's from ice cream."

Now Gary's fourteen-year-old brother, Thomas, looked up from the floor where he was taping a frayed microphone wire. He was the band's official roadie, sound man, and master van packer.

"What else could it be from?" he asked.

"You don't want to know, Tommy," Susan told him.

"Aw, don't give me that," Thomas huffed.

"Karl was insinuating that Susan might be pregnant," Gary told his little brother. "Of course, the idea is *inconceivable*."

Oscar and Susan groaned at the pun. Thomas grinned.

"I get it," he said.

Oscar bent down next to Susan in front of the broken mirror. "Excuse me, dear," he said. "Do you think I could share your dressing table for a moment?" He tilted his head down as if he was inspecting his thinning hair.

"Just think of all the time you're going to save during your life not combing your hair," Karl said from across the room. "And all the money you'll save not buying shampoo and not getting your hair cut."

Oscar turned and glared at him. "And just think, Karl, what the world would be like if everyone had a deep and penetrating mind like yours. No one would ever graduate kindergarten."

The others got a chuckle out of that. Oscar started pacing around the room again. "How much longer are they going to make us wait?" he asked.

"Not very long, Oscar," Mrs. Roesch said as she pushed open the dressing-room door and came in. Karl's mother was a tall woman with red hair like her son's. She wore old bell-bottom jeans and a denim workshirt with flowers embroidered on it. Her "hippie clothes," Karl called them.

"I just looked at the crowd," she said. "It's really filling up out there. Are you ready to start?"

Everyone began to get up. "Did you see any record company people?" Oscar asked.

Mrs. Roesch seemed to hesitate. "The place is so crowded. It's hard to tell."

"Didn't you see anyone?" Karl asked.

"Well, I might have seen someone from Blitz Records."

"Blitz Records?" Karl scowled. "What's that?"

"I think it's an independent label from Staten Island," Mrs. Roesch explained.

"Ah, Staten Island!" Oscar exclaimed. "A veritable hotbed of new rock-and-roll talent!"

Mrs. Roesch began to fidget with her handbag and pulled out a cigarette. She lit it nervously. "I tried, Oscar. I've been on the phone all week, trying to get people from the record companies to come. You don't know how hard it is. They just don't pay any attention."

Gary and Karl glanced at each other. It was just like Rick Jones said. No professional management company, no clout.

Six

Carrying his guitar, Gary left the dressing room and walked down a narrow brick hall. He made a left turn through a door and climbed up to the stage. It was pitch-black. The backstage lights were off and the stage curtain was pulled tight. All he could see were the red lights on the band's amps and faint glimmers seeping in between the curtain and the stage floor. On the other side of the curtain, he could hear the sounds of the audience—lots of voices talking at once, glasses tinkling, and chair legs scraping against the floor. The air backstage was hot and smoky, but cold pregig jitters ran through him.

The rest of the band moved across the stage to their instruments. Gary waited until they were set.

"Karl," he whispered in the darkness toward the shadowy silhouette of his drummer.

"Yeah?"

"You ready?"

Karl answered with a light tap of his snare drum and a

tentative thump on his bass drum. "A-okay," he whispered back.

Gary turned next in the direction of his cousin. "Hit an A, Susan."

Susan responded with a sharp bass note and Gary turned toward Oscar's ironing board with the synthesizer on it.

"Oscar?" Gary whispered.

There was no answer in the dark.

"Oscar?" Gary whispered again, trying to make out the figure of the keyboard player in the shadows.

Still no answer.

"*Oscar!*" Gary hissed.

"Where is he?" Karl asked.

"I don't know," Gary said, alarmed. From the other side of the curtain came the sound of footsteps across the stage. Then, the voice of the club's emcee blared out through the sound system. "*Good evening. I would like to welcome you to another night of hot rock at Shelter.*"

"Thomas," Gary hissed into the dark.

"Yeah?" came a voice from the side of the stage.

"Get Mrs. Roesch. Tell her we can't find Oscar. And hurry."

Meanwhile, the emcee was saying, "*Tonight we welcome back Gary Specter and the Coming Attractions Plus Oscar!*"

Applause and cheers erupted from the audience. But behind the curtain, Gary was wondering how to explain that tonight it would be the Coming Attractions *Minus* Oscar.

"What's the problem?" Mrs. Roesch whispered from the side of the stage.

"We can't find Oscar."

"*What!*"

"He's gone. Disappeared."

"What should we do?" There was panic in Mrs. Roesch's voice.

"I suggest you try to find him," Karl said.

While Mrs. Roesch went off to look for Oscar, the club's emcee droned on: *"Before we begin tonight's show, I'd just like to tell you what you can expect to see at Shelter in the weeks to come. . . ."*

Just keep talking, Gary prayed.

It seemed to take forever, but finally Gary heard footsteps climbing up on the stage. "Oscar?" he whispered, just barely able to make out his shape in the dark.

"Yes."

"Where have you been?"

"I'm sorry," the dark silhouette of the keyboard player said. "I just don't think I can go on tonight."

"What are you talking about?" Gary asked. "We're due to start any second now."

"I realize that," Oscar said. He stood in the dark and talked as if there was no audience out there waiting. "But I just can't go on playing in clubs like this. I know what our problem is. It's our manager. We are never going to get anywhere because she doesn't know the music business and doesn't have the right connections."

"Well, you certainly picked a great time to tell us," Susan said from the other side of the stage.

"Oscar," Karl hissed. "If you don't get behind that keyboard right now, I'll break your skull!"

"I'm sorry, Karl," Oscar said patiently. "I know she's your mother, but before she became our manager she'd never had anything to do with music. It's not her fault, but we've outgrown her."

Gary could not believe this was actually happening. Oscar couldn't quit the band just seconds before showtime.

"Look," he said. "Please play tonight. I promise we'll talk about it just as soon as the gig is over. Won't we, Susan? Karl?"

But Susan shook her head. "I don't think there's anything wrong with Mrs. Roesch," she said. "And I'm tired of Oscar acting like such a prima donna."

"Oh, great," Gary groaned. "Why don't we just all walk off the stage right now and fight about it."

"No, hold it," Karl said. "I think we better talk it over later."

"I think that's very mature of you," Oscar said.

"Just shut up and get behind the synthesizer," Karl told him.

Just at that moment, the emcee announced, *"And now, Gary Specter and the Coming Attractions Plus Oscar!"*

The audience started applauding and whistling. The curtains parted and spotlights flooded the stage. Squinting in the sudden bright light, Gary quickly looked around to make sure that Oscar had made it to the synthesizer. He had. Wonders would never cease. Gary turned, leaped into the air, and hit the first chord of the opening song. Music burst from the amps. As his eyes adjusted to the light, Gary saw that the club was jammed. The tables around the dance floor were full of people and more stood in the back. Gary smiled. A big crowd always made him feel better.

Despite the problems with Oscar, the show that night was a good one. Shelter might have been too cramped, and too smoky, but the sound system was solid and the stage was big enough for the band's rock-and-roll acrobatics. Once they got Oscar to play, they really started cooking. Karl's drums sent shock waves through the air, Susan thumped out an earthquake of bass lines, Oscar's keyboard literally shook on the ironing board, and Gary's fingers ran up and down the neck of the Stratocaster, sending sizzling licks soaring through each song.

Gary danced and strutted across the stage, slapped the palms of fans who reached up toward him, skittered and skipped, and even did a split. Susan did chorus-line kicks, and Karl twirled drumsticks in the air like batons and occasionally bounced one off the skins and into the audience.

Even Oscar got into the show. Once the music began, he forgot to be his normal grouchy self and was transformed. There was nothing he wouldn't do for the crowd.

Even after Gary, Karl, and Susan were exhausted and hoarse, Oscar still seemed as fresh as he'd been for the first song. As they came onstage for the last encore of the night, Gary carried a bottle of beer and Karl wore a towel over his shoulder. But Oscar skipped past them and onto the stage wearing a child's hat with ear flaps and carrying a huge pacifier he'd bought in a joke store.

Out in the audience, girls started to shriek. As the band took their places, the keyboard player stood at the front of the stage, illuminated by a single spotlight. The band started to play; Oscar clutched the mike and crooned:

> *"I fell in love with the baby-sitter.*
> *Now I'm older but I still can't quit her.*
> *I been in love with her since I was four—*
> *Don't say she can't stay with me no more."*

As the band joined in on the chorus, Oscar disengaged the mike from the stand and started crawling around on his hands and knees like a baby. He even sat on the stage and sucked his thumb.

> *" 'Cause she's my baby-sitter, oh yeah.*
> *She's my baby-sitter, all right.*
> *Well I may be twenty-one*
> *But we still have lots of fun.*
> *She's my baby-baby-sitter."*

Now he sat on the edge of the stage, swinging his feet and hugging the giant pacifier. Dozens of girls in the audience were really going nuts. Two muscular bouncers took positions in front of the stage to prevent them from running up and grabbing the young singer.

> *"Four bucks an hour, that's all it takes.*
> *We watch the tube and make thick shakes.*
> *We don't worry 'bout the folks comin' home*
> *'Cause I moved out years ago. Now I live all alone*
> *With my baby-sitter. . . ."*

The crowd roared. They always went berserk when Oscar sang that line. The bouncers had their hands full trying to keep girls off the stage as he did a series of clumsy forward rolls ending in a futile attempt at a three-point headstand. It was even hard for the band not to laugh at his antics, and they'd seen it all a dozen times before. Gary, Susan, and Karl looked at each other and smiled. All of the band's hassles and problems seemed far, far away.

Seven

The dressing room was a zoo that night. Somehow, dozens of fans managed to get in. Gary and the rest of the band were exhausted. They had just played, sweated, and sung their way through four hours of hard rock and the last thing they needed was a big postgig party. But they were surrounded.

"You guys were great!"

"I can't believe you haven't been signed to make an album!"

"I haven't seen a live show that entertaining since Prince!"

"Thanks, really, thanks," Gary said as he moved through the crowd, looking for a place to sit down. Meanwhile, Oscar was nearly trampled by a large contingent of cute girls. Susan was doing her best to fend off the advances of a number of tall, good-looking guys, and Karl was engulfed by a bunch of scruffy-looking pot smokers.

Even Thomas had to deal with a bunch of tough fourteen-year-olds with beer cans in their hands and cigarettes stuck behind their ears.

An attractive girl brushed close to Gary, smiled enticingly, and moved away into the crowd. Gary watched her, but made no effort to follow. It was so weird. A year ago he never would have believed that people would just want to touch him for no reason. But those things happened all the time now.

No sooner had the girl passed than out of the corner of his eye Gary saw a chubby, blond-haired guy named Charlie push his way through the crowd.

"Hey, man," Charlie said, shaking Gary's hand. "That was fab, really fab." He was wearing a black leather jacket adorned with silver chains, and baggy green Army camouflage pants; always keeping up with the latest rock styles, no matter how dumb-looking. He showed up at practically every gig the band did.

Gary was already trying to figure out how to escape when he saw that Charlie wanted him to meet another guy and two girls. The same girls he had seen at Susan's ice cream shop. One of them was the girl with the long auburn hair.

Suddenly, Gary wasn't thinking about escape anymore.

"Listen, I want you to meet a very tight buddy of mine," Charlie was telling his friends. "Gary, this is Joe Leviten, Tina Peluso, and Allison Ollquist."

Gary nodded politely, but he looked only at Allison. Right into her big brown eyes. She had very clear, pale skin, and her face was slender and as pretty as he remembered it. She was wearing tight jeans and a loose red-and-white-striped sweater.

She smiled shyly at him. Gary knew he was staring at her, but he couldn't help it. She was so attractive. What was she doing here with Charlie?

"That was some hot gig," Charlie was saying. "I swear, your band is truly awesome."

Gary managed to tear his eyes away from Allison long enough to thank him for the compliment.

Charlie gestured to his friend, Joe, a skinny guy with long curly black hair, who was also wearing a black leather jacket. The motor city twins, Gary thought.

"You know, me and Joe have a band," Charlie said. "You think we could open for you sometime?"

Gary didn't know what to say. It was just like Charlie to ask something outrageous like that.

"Or maybe we could jam with you during one of your shows," Joe suggested.

"We really don't do much jamming," Gary said, trying to be polite. "We keep the show pretty tight." He glanced at Allison again, wishing there was a way he could get to talk to her.

"You think your manager might be interested in taking on another band?" Charlie asked.

Gary could have laughed. The kid had absolutely no limits. "Well, Charlie," he said, "I think she just wants to work with us."

Charlie nodded, but Gary knew he wouldn't give up that easily. The kid was too brazen. Sure enough, Charlie excused himself from his friends and tugged him through the crowd into a corner of the room. Putting his hand on Gary's shoulder, he whispered, "I didn't want to say this in front of Joe, but if you guys ever need a rhythm guitarist, I could probably make myself available."

Just what I've always dreamed of, Gary thought. He remembered hearing Charlie play guitar once. It sounded like he had boxing gloves on. Still, Gary pretended that he deeply appreciated the offer.

"I think we'd work real well together," Charlie said.

"I'm sure we would," Gary said. "But we're not really set up for a rhythm man right now."

"I'm just saying, if you ever need one, you know?" the

kid said. "And I've got a lot of songs too. If you ever need any songs."

Gary knew he had to escape. He looked through the crowd for Mrs. Roesch, but she was nowhere in sight. Then his eye caught Karl's and he mouthed a few silent words.

The drummer understood. "All right, folks," he yelled over the crowd. "We really appreciate you coming back here tonight. But the band is tired. I think it's time to leave." He started shooing people toward the door.

Charlie realized that he was going to have to leave. "Uh, Gary," he said, "you think you could give me your phone number? Maybe I could call and talk to you some more about this."

"Well, uh . . ." Before Gary could come up with an answer, Allison came to the rescue.

"Come on, Charlie," she said, taking him by the arm. "I think we better go."

For a second her eyes met Gary's. He got the distinct impression that she knew Charlie was hassling him and was trying to help out.

Charlie allowed himself to be pulled away. "See you at the next gig, okay?" he yelled to Gary.

Gary smiled regretfully and waved good-bye.

When the door finally closed and the last fan was gone, the band collapsed wherever there was a place to sit.

"Whew, am I tired," Gary groaned as he sprawled on the old green couch.

"Me too," Karl said, sitting on the floor and lighting a cigarette. Thomas immediately bummed a butt off him and lit up too. He'd just started smoking recently, and Gary didn't like the idea much. Nor did he like him drinking beer or his surly little tough-guy attitude. But right now he was too tired to make a big deal over it.

"I noticed that Charlie found you again," Susan said as

she sat at the broken mirror, taking off her makeup with cold cream and tissues.

"Yeah, that kid is unreal," Karl said. "Did he ask you if he could join the band?"

Gary nodded.

"He got Oscar two weeks ago," Karl said. "Wouldn't leave him alone. Right, Oscar?"

Oscar didn't answer. He'd started pacing around the room again.

"Oh, Oscar, if you start complaining again, I'll scream," Susan said.

Oscar only gave her a cold look.

"I just don't understand you," Susan said. "Half an hour ago you were so into the music. You were jumping around the stage like a wildman. You didn't care who was in the audience."

"You're schizo, Oscar," Karl said.

"Maybe," Oscar grumbled. "But no record company people means no progress. You're right. During the gig I'm too busy playing to worry about who's in the audience. But after the gig I care. We put on great shows, but nobody except a couple of hundred fans knows about them. We rehearse all week and play gigs every weekend. It takes up all our time and we have nothing to show for it."

"Maybe it's just going to take more time," Susan said.

Oscar shook his head. "No, it's going to take connections. It's going to take the right people from the big clubs and the right people from the record companies. If we can't get to the heavies, we'll never get anywhere. We'll just be the best band the world never heard of."

As Oscar spoke, Gary could feel Karl and Susan looking at him for his reaction. They all had equal parts in the band, but whenever they got into a conflict like this, they eventually looked to him to resolve it. Gary pushed his hand back through his hair. He was too worn out to argue and he wasn't sure that Oscar was wrong anyway. One thing was certain, playing in dumps wasn't getting them where they needed to go. Not when bands like the Zoomies were out there making albums and touring through fifteen states.

"Okay," he told them. "We'll do something. Just give me some time to think about it."

Eight

Later that night a small crowd of fans waited outside on the sidewalk for the band. It was raining and chilly and they stood near the door of the club, holding folded newspapers over their heads or just letting the rain soak them. When Gary and the rest of the band came out, they crowded around, asking for autographs.

"Oh, Gary, please!"

"Oscar! Oscar!"

One girl even asked Gary to sign his name on her arm.

"Right on your arm?" Gary asked with a scowl.

"Yeah." The girl grinned while her friends looked at Gary and giggled.

So Gary wrote his name on her arm and when he had finished, the girl's friends crowded around her, inspecting the signature on her bare skin as if it were a rare piece of artwork. Gary shook his head. Sometimes you really had to wonder.

After the autograph seekers left, Gary and the rest of the

band climbed into the van. It seemed impossible that six people and all the equipment could be squeezed inside, but Thomas, the master van packer, had a special knack for performing such miracles. Everyone managed to wedge themselves in between the drums, amps, and guitar cases. Gary had just gotten comfortable when he smelled smoke. He turned around and saw that Thomas had a cigarette.

"Do you have to smoke in here?" he asked.

"What are you, the surgeon general?" Thomas snapped back.

"It is getting a little smoky," Susan said.

"So open a window," Thomas said.

Gary glared at him. It was bad enough that at the age of fourteen Thomas had taken up smoking and drinking, but he'd also become so totally self-centered that Gary sometimes felt like giving him a good shot in the head.

However, he restrained himself and said, "It's raining, flea brain."

Thomas looked around. It was pretty obvious that the majority in the van was against his smoking. "Okay," he said, "one last drag."

"What's the difference?" Gary asked. "You don't inhale anyway."

"Do too," Thomas said, exhaling a cloud of smoke.

"Do not," Gary said.

"Will you guys cut it out already?" Susan asked.

Mrs. Roesch put the van in gear, and Gary looked out the rain-streaked window and saw the last of the band's fans walking down the sidewalk. It still amazed him that fans stayed late after a show to ask for autographs. And yet he used to do it too. It was just hard to believe that the Coming Attractions were a band that people would want autographs from. Somehow, he'd always figured that when a band got to the autographing stage, their problems would be over.

The rain drummed steadily on the roof of the van. As Mrs. Roesch slowed down to make a turn, the van's head-lights caught two girls standing in the rain on the dark street corner.

"Stop the van, Mrs. Roesch!" he shouted.

"What?" Mrs. Roesch said. "Why, Gary?"

"Please stop," Gary insisted.

"What's going on?" Susan asked.

Gary was already reaching for the door handle. "Just wait here a second," he said. "I'll be right back." He pushed the door open and jumped down onto the wet pavement. The two girls were still standing on the corner about half a block away and Gary jogged through the rain toward them.

"Hey!" he yelled.

They turned quickly. It was Allison and Tina, and they were getting drenched by the rain.

"What are you doing out here?" Gary asked. He could feel the cold rain start to soak down his hair.

"Trying to find a cab," Tina said. Black eyeliner ran down her cheeks.

"You want a ride with us?" Gary asked, pointing up the block toward the van.

The two girls looked at each other. Gary could see that they weren't certain.

"What do you think?" Tina asked Allison.

Allison seemed to hesitate. Even standing in the dark with her wet hair hanging like strings on her shoulders, she looked pretty.

"You're just going to catch pneumonia out here," Gary said. And so would he, he thought, feeling the rain start to seep through his jacket.

Allison looked at him uncertainly. Suddenly there was a loud crack of thunder and it started to rain even harder.

"Oh, come on, Allison," Tina said. "We can't stand here all night."

But Allison still resisted.

"Hey," Gary said. "Do I look like the kind of guy who goes around kidnapping people?"

Despite the downpour, Allison brushed some wet hair off her face and smiled slightly at him. "On a scale of one to ten I'd give you a four."

Thunder boomed again and a huge crack of lightning burst through the dark sky. Tina jumped. "Forget it, Allison," she said. "I'm going. You can wait for a cab all night if you want."

Allison looked back down the street and then up at the van. "Okay," she said. "You've convinced me."

The three of them ran down the sidewalk to the van and Gary pulled open the back door. "Hey, can we make some room back here?" he shouted inside. "We have some guests."

Everyone groaned.

"Aw, come on, Gary, it's too crowded," Thomas said.

But Gary was already helping Allison and Tina into the van. "What would you want me to do?" Gary asked his little brother. "Leave them out in the rain?"

Thomas shrugged and didn't answer. Everyone squeezed around to make room. Gary climbed in and pulled the door shut behind him.

"Can we go now?" Mrs. Roesch asked.

"Sure," Gary said. He wedged his back against an amplifier. Across from him, Allison and Tina were squeezed in between Oscar and a couple of guitar cases. Thomas had climbed up behind them and was lying across the bass drum box and another amp. Everyone was sitting with their knees scrunched up to their chests.

Mrs. Roesch put the van in gear and it lurched forward. In the back, Gary made introductions. "Tina and Allison, this is Susan, Thomas, Karl, and Oscar."

"Welcome to the sardine can," Oscar grumbled.

"So where can we take you?" Gary asked.

"Well, we don't want you to go out of your way," Allison said. "Where are you going?"

"Nowhere," Oscar said. "We just like to pretend we're refugees and drive around all night in the rain with no room to breathe."

"Don't pay any attention to him," Gary told Allison. "We're going up to Seventy-eighth Street. But we can take you home. It'll be no trouble. Really."

"Seventy-eighth will be fine," Allison said. "Right, Tina?"

"Sure," Tina said.

"You live around there?" Gary asked.

"Not far away," Allison said. Apparently she didn't want to say exactly where.

The van bounced uptown with everyone bracing themselves against the equipment. Nobody else had much to say. They all seemed tired and weary. Except Gary. Suddenly he felt wide awake. He couldn't explain it, but every time he looked across at Allison, or caught her eye or smiled at her, his insides started to buzz. It was the weirdest feeling.

"What happened to Charlie and his friend?" he asked.

The two girls glanced at each other. "We ditched them," Tina said.

"How come?" Gary asked.

"Charlie wanted us to go to his house," Tina said. "We knew his parents weren't home."

"We suspected their intentions," Allison added.

"How'd you know Charlie in the first place?"

"Tina and Joe are cousins," Allison said.

"I'd say *distant* cousins after tonight," Tina added.

"You go to the clubs much?" Gary asked.

Tina and Allison shook their heads.

"How come?"

"They're too grungy and crowded," Tina said. "And guys are always trying to pick us up."

I can see why, Gary thought.

"What did you think of the music?" Karl asked from his seat in the front.

"It was okay," Tina said.

"Just okay?" Karl asked.

"Didn't you like it?" Gary asked Allison.

"It was good," she said. But Gary got the feeling that she wasn't a real rock-and-roll fan.

"What about the show?" Oscar asked.

"I thought it was very entertaining," Allison said.

"Damn right it's entertaining," Thomas said. "They're the best damn band in the whole damn city."

"Learn a new word, Tommy?" Susan asked.

"Go stuff yourself," he replied.

They continued uptown and stopped at 78th Street. It wasn't raining as hard now and Gary hopped out and held the door for the two girls. He had an idea.

"It's pretty late," he said. "Maybe I better walk you home."

"Oh, no, that's okay," Allison said, turning up the collar of her jacket. "Thanks for the ride. I really appreciate it."

"Me too," said Tina.

"You sure you want to walk home alone?" Gary asked.

"It's only a short walk," Allison said. "We'll make it all right."

Gary shrugged, disappointed. "Well, okay."

Allison smiled. "Thanks again for the ride." Then she and Tina turned and started to walk away quickly in the dark.

For a moment, Gary stood on the sidewalk and watched them.

"Uh-hum!" Someone in the van cleared their throat. "We're waiting, Gary."

"Yeah, I know." Gary climbed back into the van and closed the door. He was already trying to figure out how he could get to see Allison again.

Nine

The applause was thunderous! Gary stood on the stage of Madison Square Garden, gasping at the huge crowd of cheering, screaming fans. It was incredible! Fantastic! A dream come true! They filled the floor before him and then rose in endless banks of seats spreading outward and upward around the giant sports arena. Thousands and thousands of delirious applauding fans!

Glowing with pride, Gary turned and introduced the other members of the band. The deafening applause grew even louder as he pointed to Oscar, who had somehow grown a full head of thick brown hair. The applause grew louder still as Gary nodded to Karl, whose complexion had magically cleared up. When Gary introduced Susan, the cheering was so loud, he thought he would go deaf.

"GARY! GARY! GARY!" The crowd began to shout his name in a single giant voice. Gary was stunned. He had never experienced such a tribute!

"GARY! GARY! GARY!" They surged forward. Hundreds of fans climbing up on the stage and swarming around the band, literally lifting Gary and the other band members onto their shoulders. Gary felt himself rise into the air. He looked down and saw hundreds of beaming faces.

But one face stood out. It was Allison! She was on the edge of the crowd, trying to get closer, but the mass of bodies was too thick. Gary started to struggle against all the hands and shoulders between them, trying to fight his way down to the ground, but it seemed impossible.

"GARY! GARY! GARY!" They were carrying him away. Gary kept fighting, but there were too many of them. Soon Allison was no longer visible in the sea of faces around him.

"Gary! Gary!" Someone was knocking on his door. "Wake up, Mr. Rock Star!"

Gary woke with a start. It had been a dream. Only a dream! What weirdness.

The knocking continued on his door. "Telephone call for his highness, Mr. Rock Star."

Gary sat up, shaking his head, still woozy. "Okay, okay, I hear you!" he yelled. But instead of getting out of bed he closed his eyes for one second more and pictured Allison again. Only now that he was half awake he could make the dream end the way he wanted it to, with the crowds departing, leaving him and Allison on the empty stage, in a vast, empty Madison Square Garden. Just him and Allison, alone. . . .

"Did you have a nice sleep, dear?" his mother asked through the door, abruptly ending his fantasy. Gary opened his eyes and swung his legs over the edge of the bed.

"Do you get some kind of perverse satisfaction out of waking me up every day?" he yelled at the door.

"Temper, temper."

Gary sighed. He got up; pulled on a pair of jeans; went

out into the hall; marched right past his mother and down to the kitchen. He picked up the phone.

"Yeah?"

"Rise and shine, sleeping beauty."

"Oh, hi, Karl," Gary said, yawning. "What's up?"

"From the sound of it, you're not," Karl said.

Gary scratched his head and wondered if there was some kind of conspiracy against letting him sleep past two in the afternoon. "Do you have something to tell me, or do you just enjoy hearing me yawn?" he asked, yawning again.

"Remember that guy, Barney Star?" Karl asked. "The one we met at the Multigram Building?"

"Yeah, the guy in the suit and cowboy boots," Gary said.

"Well, I called him up this morning," Karl said. "He told us we could call up if we wanted just to talk things over."

"Sure, so what did he say?"

"Uh, I invited him to come hear us rehearse tonight," Karl said.

"You what?" Gary felt himself take three giant steps toward being fully awake.

"I figured it couldn't hurt," Karl said. "I mean, we're not obligated to him or anything."

"Yeah, but Karl, there are four people in this band and we all have equal say on something like that," Gary said. "Don't you think you should have asked the rest of us first?"

"I thought about it and I figured that deep down the rest of you would probably want him to come, too, but you'd never say so because you'd be afraid you'd hurt my feelings because of my mother and everything."

"She is our manager, Karl."

"I'm not saying she isn't," Karl said. "I'm just saying, let's hear what this guy has to say. It's not gonna cost us anything."

Gary wasn't certain. "You sure you want to do this, Karl?

If it ever gets back to your mother, it could really screw things up with her and us."

Karl was quiet for a second and then he said, "I know it, man."

"And you still want Star to come tonight?" Gary asked.

"Listen, I think it's come to the point where we have to ask ourselves why we're in this dumb band," the drummer said. "Is it for us or for her?"

"Well, when you come right down to it, it's for us," Gary said.

"Then we better have Star come tonight."

Ten

Normally, the trip to the rehearsal studio did not take Gary past the Ripton School. But that day he took a new route. Resting his guitar case on the sidewalk, he paused in front of the school and watched a steady stream of girls flow out the big wooden doors as the bells rang, ending the school day. Would Allison be one of them?

Sure enough, a few moments later Gary saw her come out of the school, wearing a heavy gray turtleneck sweater and pink leg warmers. Under one arm she was carrying a blue nylon bag, and her long reddish brown hair was pulled into a ponytail. He watched as she skipped lightly down the steps. But instead of going down the sidewalk as he expected, she cut across the street. Straight toward him.

Suddenly Gary didn't know what to do. He picked up his guitar case and looked around, trying to decide which direction to go in. There was a traffic light to his right so he headed toward it and waited impatiently for the "Don't

Walk" sign to change. The last thing he needed was for Allison to catch him spying on her.

Then he heard her voice: "Gary?"

Too late, he thought. He turned and tried to act surprised. "Oh, Allison, what are you doing here?"

Allison pointed back toward Ripton. "I just got out of school. What are you doing here?"

"Uh, I was just waiting for the light to change." As he spoke, the traffic signal changed from "Don't Walk" to "Walk."

"It just changed," Allison said.

Gary looked up at the traffic light and back at Allison.

She gave him a funny look. "Aren't you going to cross?"

"Are you?" Gary asked.

"No, I'm going that way." Allison pointed up Second Avenue.

"Hmm, I could probably go that way too," Gary said.

"But it's the opposite direction from the way you're going," Allison said.

Gary picked up his guitar case. "Well," he said. "I can probably go either way." He pointed in both directions.

Allison squinted at him and grinned. "Are you putting me on?"

"Absolutely not," Gary said. "Come on." He and Allison began to walk up Second Avenue. Now what? he thought. Come on, dummy, think of something to say. He glanced at her dance bag.

"So you're a dancer, huh?" he said.

"I like to dance," Allison said. "I'm not sure how much of a dancer that makes me."

"What kind of dancing do you do?" Gary asked.

"Classical ballet," Allison said.

"Oh, yeah, like *Swan Lake*, right?"

Allison smiled. "Yes, like *Swan Lake*."

As they walked down the sidewalk, Gary could feel that

Allison was wary of him. She was acting polite and distant. The way you did when you were with a stranger. Was it because guys tried to pick her up all the time? Or was it because she only knew him as a rock-and-roller who strutted across club stages gyrating his hips provocatively?

"You know, this may sound dumb," he said, "but I think rock and roll and classical ballet probably have more similarities than most people realize."

"Why?" Allison asked.

"Because they both require acting," Gary said. "I mean, if you're in a rock band you have to act like this maniac stud onstage, and if you're in a ballet you act like a perfectly tuned human machine in total control. But when a rock star comes off the stage he's just another human being, just the way a ballerina is offstage."

Allison glanced at him and smiled. "I wouldn't know. I've never been on stage."

"But you can understand what I'm talking about right?" Gary asked.

Allison nodded. "Yes. And I'll be sure to keep it in mind the next time I meet a ballerina, or a rock star."

Gary got the feeling that she wasn't taking him seriously. He felt like a fool, tagging along next to her, trying to make conversation. But he couldn't help it. Something kept pushing him forward. It was almost like she'd cast a magic spell over him.

They walked another block and then Allison stopped. "We're here."

"Where?" Gary asked.

"At my dance class," she said, pointing up to the second floor.

Gary looked up and through the windows saw some girls in colorful tights, stretching and bending.

"Thanks for walking with me," Allison said. "I hope it didn't take you too far out of your way."

"Uh, no, of course not," Gary said, looking around and realizing that he was now many blocks from the subway. If he didn't hurry, he'd be late for rehearsal.

"Well, good-bye," Allison said. She turned and started to go into the building.

"Wait," Gary said.

Allison stopped, and looked at him.

"How often do you take ballet class?" he asked.

"Almost every day. Why?"

Gary could feel a foolish grin forming on his face. "Uh, just wondering, that's all. Have a good class."

Allison turned and went inside and Gary stood on the sidewalk and watched until she'd disappeared up the stairs. Then he turned and started walking quickly toward the subway. What had come over him? He felt he'd acted like a complete fool and yet he couldn't help himself. The more reserved Allison was, the more he wanted to get to know her. There was just something about her—the way she looked, the way she was—that made him feel a little crazy, but good. He knew he wanted to see her again. Soon.

Eleven

That night Barney Star came to the rehearsal studio and told them he could get them gigs at the Bottom Line and DeLux. He said he could get them an album contract and a tour. After he had left, the band held a meeting and voted three to one to hire him on a trial basis. Susan was the sole dissenter.

Later, Gary and Susan walked home from the studio carrying their guitars. It was getting colder and Gary noticed that people were beginning to wear their down jackets and coats. November was just a week away. For him and Susan it would be the first November in fourteen years with no school.

"I really get the feeling that the three of you don't want Mrs. Roesch anymore because she's a woman," Susan was saying. "If she were a man, I don't think you'd be so eager to dump her for this Barney Star character."

Gary shook his head. "First of all, I'm not sure I do want to dump her, Sue. We've only agreed to use Star on a trial basis. I hope Mrs. Roesch won't even find out until we can see whether Star really comes through or not."

"I can't believe you agreed to keep it a secret from her," Susan said as they waited at a corner for the light to change.

Gary pushed his hand through his hair and took a deep breath of cold air. "Listen, Sue, I know you think it's dishonest, but right now it's hard enough for me just to keep the band together. Oscar was ready to quit if we didn't try Star. To tell you the truth, I think we're all really disappointed by the way things have been going. If Star really can help, we'd be crazy not to let him."

"Even if it means lying to Mrs. Roesch," Susan said.

Gary had no answer to that. He just kept imagining the alternative: month after month of playing in little clubs, the band never getting anywhere.

They crossed a few more streets and came to a dark block around the corner from where they lived. There were a couple of vacant lots and a deserted school yard where gangs sometimes hung out. As they walked down the block, Gary became aware of the sound of Led Zeppelin music coming from the school yard. A little farther up he could see a group of guys hanging around, smoking cigarettes.

Gary motioned Susan to cross to the other side of the street. As they passed the yard, Gary suddenly stopped.

"What is it, Gary?" Susan asked.

"Am I seeing things, or is that Thomas?"

Susan looked across at the group. There was a kid who looked an awful lot like Thomas, wearing an old denim jacket with the sleeves ripped out and a hooded sweat shirt underneath. If it was Thomas, it was way past the time he was allowed to be outside at night alone.

Gary went back across the street toward the group. Now he was certain that the kid in the sleeveless denim jacket was his brother.

"Hey, Thomas," he said.

The gang of kids grew silent and looked at Gary. Then Thomas said, "Yeah?"

"Could you come over here a minute?" Gary said. "I want to talk to you."

Thomas took his time leaving the group and sauntered over slowly. "What is it?" he said, sticking his hands in his back pockets and trying to look cool.

"What are you doing here?" Gary asked in a low voice the other kids couldn't hear. "You know you're not allowed out this late on a weeknight."

"Mom sent me to get some milk," Thomas answered in a whisper.

"Well, you better go get it and go home," Gary told him.

Thomas made a face and strolled back toward the gang. Gary and Susan started to leave, but as they did, they heard him tell the others, "My brother wants me to help him fix his stereo system. See ya later."

Twelve

Each afternoon that week Gary waited outside the Ripton School for Allison and then walked her to ballet class. He planned to ask her to the band's gig at the Lounge that weekend, but he wanted to wait until he knew her better. Unfortunately, it wasn't easy to get to know someone when you only walked four or five blocks with them each day.

On Friday afternoon they arrived at the ballet school. The week was over and Gary still had not mentioned the Lounge. Just as she'd done every afternoon that week, Allison turned to say good-bye.

"Uh . . ." Gary was still uncertain about asking her. But he had to think of something fast or he'd lose the chance. "You think I could come up and watch?" he asked, gesturing toward the second floor of the building.

Allison looked surprised. "Well, I guess you could. But do you really want to?"

"Sure."

"We're not very good. I think you'll get bored."

"If I do, I'll leave," Gary said.

For a few seconds Allison looked as if she were trying to figure him out. Gary knew that she had grown less wary of him since the beginning of the week. Not that she greeted him with open arms and kisses or anything, but he knew he had made some progress.

She smiled slightly and nodded. "Okay, if you really want to." She turned and Gary followed her inside and up the stairs to the second floor.

There were eight girls, including Allison, in the class, plus the instructor and a middle-aged lady with glasses and gray hair who played the piano. Gary sat against a wall in the back of the room and watched the instructor, a small muscular man with short curly black hair who wore black leotards. He led the girls through the dance routine and yelled at them in a shrill voice. Gary had never watched ballet closely before and he was amazed at how controlled the dancers' bodies were. It reminded him of the body control good basketball players developed—the ability to fly and twist and almost change directions in midair. Some of these girls would probably be pretty good on a basketball court, he thought.

The instructor kept repeating the same dance steps over and over and Gary found himself settling back comfortably, almost mesmerized by the rhythms of the dancers and the piano music. The air had a certain light odor, sort of a mixture of sweat and perfume, that Gary had never smelled before. Girlish sweat, he decided. He watched Allison for a while. She seemed totally concentrated on the dance and never even looked in his direction.

Gary didn't mind. He was perfectly happy just to sit there and watch. All week long he'd found that he liked her more and more. She wasn't loud or pushy or stuck-up. She was talkative, but she also listened and didn't laugh when he made an idiot of himself (which seemed to happen at least once during each walk). She didn't seem neurotic or weird or anything like that. The only things that bothered him were that she seemed to resist getting too friendly, and she didn't know a lot about rock—problems that could be overcome.

Gary listened to the piano music and the padding of feet, the grunts and groans of the dancers, the shrill instructions of the ballet teacher. His thoughts began to drift elsewhere —whoever thought having a rock band could mean so many hassles? He felt like everybody was pulling at him. His mother, Oscar, Barney Star, Karl, Susan. And if things weren't already bad enough, his little brother was becoming a punk. All because he had one simple dream, one simple idea that he cherished: to be a rock musician. Was it so much to ask for? Was it so impossible to ask for?

For some crazy reason he started thinking about Christopher Columbus. What if the world really had been flat? Then Columbus wouldn't have been a hero, he would have been some fool who sailed off the earth's edge and was never heard from again. The thing was, nobody really knew what the earth's shape was until Columbus took the gamble and went to sea. The same was true with the band. Everybody had an opinion, but nobody *really* knew. The only way you could find out was by trying it yourself, by taking the gamble yourself.

"I can't believe you're still here." Sometime later Allison's words snapped Gary out of his thoughts. She was standing over him, wiping her forehead with a towel.

"Uh . . ."

"You're a daydreamer," Allison said.

"Well, I . . ."

"It's okay," she said. "So am I. I daydream about being the principal dancer with the American Ballet Company at Lincoln Center. What do you daydream about?"

Gary looked up at her and grinned sheepishly. "Me and my band playing eight sold-out nights at Madison Square Garden."

Allison nodded. She was one of the few people who didn't look at him like he was crazy when he said something like that. Now she put her hands in the small of her back and bent backward, grimacing slightly.

"Tired?" Gary asked.

"The bulge really worked us today," Allison said.

"The bulge?" Gary asked.

Allison motioned toward the dancing instructor, who was standing across the room, talking to one of the dancers. "That's his nickname," she said. "You know, the tights."

Gary felt his face turn red.

"Are you blushing?" Allison asked him.

"Well, uh, I mean, uh, I guess I am," Gary said.

"I suppose I did, too, the first time someone called him that. But you have to admit, it fits."

"Uh . . ."

Allison shook her head. "You know, I've never met anyone who spent as much time going uh, er, well, uh, huh as you," she said. "You haven't scrambled your brains on drugs, have you?"

Gary put a finger in his mouth and crossed his eyes. "Duh . . . I . . . uh . . . don't . . . er . . . think . . . so."

"Good. Do you want to wait just a few more minutes while I cool off?" Allison asked.

"Well . . . I . . . uh . . . er . . . guess . . . huh."

After dance class Gary walked Allison home.

"I have to admit that I never really thought of rock-and-roll musicians as being serious," she said as they walked down a block lined with brownstones and bare, leafless trees. "Most of the boys I know either don't care what they do with their lives or have already decided to be lawyers and doctors. It's amazing to meet someone who actually has a mind of his own."

Gary smiled.

"But isn't it hard?" Allison asked. "I mean, don't your parents worry about you not going to college?"

"Sure, but they can't stop me," Gary said. "How could they?"

"I don't know," Allison said. "I'm sure my parents would find a way to stop me if I did anything like that."

They arrived at Allison's building, a big, fancy-looking place on Park Avenue. It was dark and cold, and Gary had zipped his leather jacket up to the neck. They stood on the sidewalk outside and watched as a long black limousine pulled up in front. Under the building's awning a doorman wearing a green uniform held open a large shiny brass door for a man in a dinner jacket and a woman wearing a fur coat over a long dress.

Gary was still trying to get up the nerve to ask Allison to come to hear him at the Lounge. He felt his mouth open and saw Allison look at him expectantly.

"So, do you go to dance class over the weekend too?" he asked.

"Sometimes on Saturday," Allison said. "When I don't have anything better to do."

Gary felt his nerves start to buzz. If that wasn't a hint, he didn't know what was. Come on, you jerk, he thought, this is the chance you've been waiting for all week!

"Uh, would you like to come see our show on Saturday night?" he asked.

"Sure," Allison replied.

Gary felt incredibly relieved. "Well, great," he said. "We're playing at this place called the Lounge. We'll probably start around ten and play until two. That's not too late, is it?"

Allison shook her head. "I think I can arrange it."

They smiled at each other as if they were glad the date had been so easy to arrange. Then Allison began to look a little embarrassed. "I better go in. So I'll see you Saturday night." She turned away.

Gary stood on the sidewalk and watched while the doorman held the door for Allison to pass through. "Good evening, Miss Ollquist," he said.

Inside, Allison turned and waved to him. Gary waved back and turned toward home.

Thirteen

A couple of hours after midnight on Saturday the members of the Coming Attractions stood offstage at the Lounge, listening to the loud applause. As shouts of *"More! More! More!"* came from the audience, Gary rolled a cold beer bottle back and forth across his forehead, trying to cool down. Next to him, Oscar wiped his face with a towel and Mrs. Roesch was blow-drying Susan's sweat-dampened hair.

"It's been a great show," Mrs. Roesch was saying. "Just great."

Gary nodded and felt a pang of guilt. He'd been feeling that way ever since the band agreed to go with Barney Star on a trial basis. Of course, Mrs. Roesch still didn't know.

The chants of *"More! More! More!"* were coming faster now, accompanied by rhythmic foot stomping.

"Ready for your encore?" Mrs. Roesch asked.

"As soon as Karl gets out of the bathroom," Gary said.

"Here he comes," Oscar said. A second later Karl came down the hall wiping his hands on his jeans.

"You think they could at least put paper towels in the men's room," he said in disgust.

"Okay, let's go," Gary said, picking up his guitar and climbing back on the stage. As soon as the crowd saw him, they began to whistle and cheer. Gary waved back and plugged his guitar into his amp. While the rest of the band followed, he tried to peer into the audience for Allison's face. But if she was there, he couldn't see her.

He glanced back at the band and then pressed his lips against the mike. "Uh-one and uh-two and uh-three!"

They hit some opening chords and the spotlights burst on, glaring straight down into their eyes. The volume was thunderous. Karl's drums were exploding. Susan blasted out a hurricane of bass notes and Oscar's keyboard shook with intensity. Gary threw himself into the song:

> *"You're having a party, but things are kind of*
> *slow.*
> *Nobody's dancing, the music's too low.*
> *So turn up the volume, then turn it up some more.*
> *Get your friends up on their feet*
> *and stompin' on the floor."*

Susan, Karl, and Oscar joined in for the chorus:

> *"Turn it up! Turn it up!*
> *Roll up those old rugs.*
> *Turn it up! Turn it up!*
> *Buy the neighbors some earplugs.*
> *Turn it up! Turn it up!*
> *There's no such thing as too high.*
> *Turn it up! Turn it up!*
> *Make that stereo cry!"*

Gary slid away from the mike and played a sizzling riff on his guitar. Sweat was rolling down his forehead. The

spotlights were hot and glared in his eyes, but he felt loose
and full of energy. The dance floor was crowded and people
in the audience were clapping to the music. Gary grinned as
his fingers raced quickly up and down the neck of his guitar.
Everybody was happy, everybody was into the music. This
was what it was all about. He jumped back to the mike for
the next verse:

> *"You're on the highway,*
> * there's a traffic jam for miles.*
> *Don't bother getting ticked off,*
> * it's only one of life's trials.*
> *Just flip on that radio*
> * and make that music play.*
> *Pretty soon it won't matter*
> * if you're stuck in that jam all day."*

Gary let go of his guitar and started clapping his hands
above his head, urging the whole crowd to join in. Pretty
soon he not only had them all clapping, but singing "Turn it
up!" as the band shouted out the chorus:

> *"Turn it up! Turn it up!*
> *Don't worry about blowing the speakers.*
> *Turn it up! Turn it up!*
> *They're just an old pair of squeakers.*
> *Turn it up! Turn it up!*
> *Don't think about the date you're missin'.*
> *Turn it up! Turn it up!*
> *Invite the girls in the next car to listen!"*

The band charged into a longer break. Oscar's fingers
were all over the synthesizer and the ironing board shook
precariously. Meanwhile, on the other side of the stage,

Susan drove a bass line while doing chorus-line kicks. And behind them all, Karl kept up a steady thunder of drum beats.

Then Gary ran back to the microphone:

> *"You're home alone,*
>   *you forgot to make a date.*
> *Your parents have gone out*
>   *and they won't be home till late.*
> *So you get out your ax and*
>   *start fooling around.*
> *Till you get it just right with those*
>   *really funky sounds."*

The audience was going berserk. There was nothing the band loved more than leading a crowd into this kind of semi-controlled insanity. The hell with the music business. The hell with A and R men who thought they were gods. None of that meant a thing as they chanted:

> *"Turn it up! Turn it up!*
> *Let it rock you to your toes.*
> *Turn it up! Turn it up!*
> *Who knows how high it really goes.*
> *Turn it up! Turn it up!*
> *'Cause, people, this is the whole deal.*
> *THE LOUDER IT GETS, THE BETTER*
>   *WE FEEL!"*

They roared into the last break, the band building the volume louder and louder until it was almost deafening. The whole place was on its feet. Oscar left his keyboards and stood at the stage's edge holding a mike stand over his head, shouting:

"Turn it up! Turn it up!
Hey, gimme more bass.
Turn it up! Turn it up!
Blow me into outer space.
Turn it up! Turn it up!
You know we're never gonna tire.
Turn it up! Turn it up!
As long as the volume gets higher!"

The crowd gave them a standing ovation as Gary and the band made their final bows and the house lights went on through the club. Mrs. Roesch was right. It had been a great show.

There'd been only one discouraging note in the night for Gary, and that was not seeing Allison. Still, he was hopeful. The place had been so jammed that he could easily have missed her. There was only one way he could know for sure. So, instead of going back to the dressing room with the rest of the band, he veered off into the crowd.

Allison wasn't sitting at any of the tables near the stage, so Gary pushed toward the bar in the back. He didn't have much hope of finding her there. The bars at rock clubs were usually the domain of single guys who were more interested in meeting girls than listening to music, and the smoke around the bar at the Lounge was so thick, Gary's eyes began to burn. By that time of night the only guys left hanging around there were either really hard up or just too drunk to make a serious attempt at leaving.

Gary was just about to give up the search when he saw something that made him freeze. There was Allison, leaning against the bar not four feet away from him. But what shocked him was that there was a guy leaning against the bar with her.

For several seconds Gary didn't move. Allison was wearing

black tights, a short red dress and a sheepskin jacket. Leaning against the bar, holding a glass in her hand, she hardly resembled a classic Ripton girl. The guy she was talking to was facing her with his back to Gary. It was obvious that he wasn't a regular at the Lounge. Most of the regulars went in for the latest punked-out clothes and hairstyles, but the guy talking to Allison was wearing a suit.

Gary wasn't sure what to do next. He assumed that if Allison had come to the Lounge, it was to see him and his band. But what if this guy was her boyfriend? Some college guy she'd just "forgotten" to mention? The idea almost made Gary sick. No, he told himself, it couldn't be. She couldn't do that to him. Could she?

There was only one way to find out. As he stepped toward them he could hear the guy tell Allison, "I make stars out of people. They're nothing when they come to me and when they leave, they're famous."

Wait a minute, Gary thought. That voice sounded familiar. The next thing he knew, Allison noticed him. She smiled broadly, reached for his arm, and pulled him toward her.

"Oh, Gary, I loved the show," she said.

"Uh, thanks, Allison," Gary said. He was close to total shock. The guy Allison was talking to was none other than Barney Star. For a moment both of them were speechless with surprise.

"Gary, you know Barney," Allison said. "He was just telling me that he's going to be your new manager."

Barney had a grin on his face that was a mile wide. "I, uh, just stopped in to catch the show, Gary. It was dynamite. Just dynamite."

But Gary wasn't fooled. Not only had Barney been trying to pick up Allison, he realized, but where did he get off telling her that he was going to manage the band?

Barney must have sensed Gary's anger because he quickly said, "You mean you two know each other? Hey, how could

I have possibly known? I really owe you both an apology. I mean, I was just trying to make some small talk, right? I mean, I never knew."

Allison nodded, but she continued to squeeze Gary's arm tightly.

"So, uh, that was really an incredible show," Barney said. "I mean, awesome. If we could get some of that on tape, we'd have a contract in no time. I'm telling you."

Gary nodded, but he was still annoyed. "Listen, Barney," he said. "No one said you were definitely managing us yet. I thought we agreed that we wanted to see what you could do for us first."

"Hey, man, don't get me wrong," Barney said. His glasses made him look like a big grinning frog. "I was just telling Allison here how much *I'd like to* manage you. I mean, you guys have supremo talent. It would be an honor if you'd allow me to represent you."

Gary felt himself relax a little. He was glad Allison was getting to hear this. "So you liked the show, huh?"

"Like it? It was fabulous, man. I mean, you have monster potential. Monster." Barney paused and lit one of his thin cigars. "You tell me what you want. Multirecord deals? Sports cars? Houses on the beach? You want the Garden? The Spectrum? You got it. Six months from now you'll be able to pick up the phone and tell some record company president you want a private jet to fly your grandmother to Miami Beach for the weekend and you'll get it."

Gary smiled. If nothing else, Barney sure had an imagination.

"So, listen," Barney said. "I told your drummer Karl that I was gonna start working on a couple of possibilities for you. Now that I've seen your act, I have some solid ideas. You'll be hearing from me soon, I promise." He held his hand out and Gary shook it. Barney patted him on the shoulder. "Hey, man, sorry about hitting on your old lady, okay? I just didn't know."

"It's okay," Gary said.

Barney grinned. "All right, gotta split. One of my bands is pulling an all-night recording session in midtown. They're so hot that the record company has security guards crawling all over the place to make sure no one walks off with any tapes. It's unreal. See ya." He turned and disappeared into the crowd.

Gary looked at Allison. "Well, I guess you just met Barney Star."

"It was a delight," Allison said. She let go of Gary's arm and put her drink down on the bar. Gary noticed that it was still full.

"Well," he said. "We better get out to the van before they leave without us." He turned around and reached for Allison's hand. As she slipped her hand into his, he could feel his heart beating like a snare drum.

Fourteen

Later that night Mrs. Roesch stopped the van at the corner of 78th and Third Avenue and Gary and Allison got out.

As the van started away again, Karl stuck his head out of the window and shouted, "Hey, don't do anything I wouldn't do!"

Gary turned and looked at Allison in the dark. She was giggling.

They started walking down the dark, quiet street. It was chilly again tonight—winter was definitely on its way. Allison pulled the collar of her sheepskin jacket up around her neck. Gary looked at his watch. "Aren't your parents going to start wondering where you are?" he asked.

"I told them I'd be out late," Allison said, pulling her jacket closed.

"They don't mind?"

"They don't love the idea," Allison said. "But they trust me."

They got to the corner of Lexington and 78th. All the

stores and restaurants were locked up, but there was still a lot of traffic on the street. In New York the traffic never stopped. A few blocks down, Gary saw a brightly lit coffee shop. "Want to go there?" he asked.

Allison hesitated and shivered a little. "We can go to my house, but we'll have to be quiet."

"You sure?" Gary asked.

"Well, if we're really quiet," Allison said.

They started walking toward Allison's building. Even though Gary was used to being up that late, he still didn't like walking around on the streets at that hour. It was an invitation to be mugged. He was relieved to see that Allison walked quickly.

"So what did you think of the show tonight?" Gary asked, walking quickly beside her in the dark.

"I thought you were very good," Allison said.

"Do you like rock music any more now?" he asked.

"I never said I hated it, Gary."

"But don't you like classical music?" Gary said. "I mean, that's what you dance to."

"In class I dance to it," Allison said. "But sometimes at home if I'm just practicing or exercising by myself, I like to listen to rock."

"Oh, yeah?" Gary was glad to hear that. "What groups do you like?"

Allison thought for a moment. "Well, I don't really pay that much attention to the names of the bands. I think I like the Usual Suspects."

"Yeah, they're good," Gary said.

"And there's a new band I just heard recently," Allison said.

"Who?" Gary asked.

"I can't remember their name," Allison said, "but they've got a great lead guitarist and one of their songs goes something like, 'Turn it up, turn it up.' "

Gary laughed. "Oh, yeah, that's uh, what's their name."

They got to Allison's and were let in by a sleepy looking doorman wearing a green uniform with gold buttons. "Good evening, Miss Ollquist," he said, trying to stifle a yawn.

Gary and Allison walked through the lobby and got into a wood-paneled elevator run by an old, thin, white-haired man in a frayed black suit. He scrutinized Gary carefully.

"Out late, Miss Ollquist," the old man said to Allison, making no effort to hide the disapproval in his voice. He pushed a lever forward and the elevator lurched upward.

Allison smiled politely at him. "How are you tonight, Mr. Green?"

"No better, no worse," Mr. Green replied acidly. The elevator stopped and the old man opened the doors. "Should I wait, Miss Ollquist?" he asked, still giving Gary the evil eye.

"No, thanks, Mr. Green," Allison said. "We'll call for you when we want you."

"It's awfully late to be inviting in company, isn't it, Miss Ollquist?" Mr. Green asked with a frown.

Allison sighed. "I appreciate your concern, Mr. Green," she said, as she searched her pockets for the keys to the apartment.

Mr. Green grumbled something Gary couldn't understand and slammed the elevator door closed. Gary looked around and found himself in a small room, sort of like a foyer. Meanwhile, Allison found her keys and unlocked the door.

"What's with that guy?" Gary asked.

Allison brought her fingers to her lips and whispered. "He thinks he's my surrogate father. He's known me since I was this big." She reached down and placed her hand about a foot from the floor.

"Real friendly type," Gary whispered.

"Just overprotective, like everyone else," Allison said, quietly pushing the door open. Inside there was a light on in the hall and Allison walked in with Gary following her. The hallway was wide and high and lined with paintings. Gary knew he'd never been in an apartment like this before. He followed Allison in and out of a series of rooms until they wound up in a kitchen. Only this kitchen was nearly half the size of his parents' whole apartment.

"We have to be quiet," Allison said in a low voice. "My father is a very light sleeper."

"Do you mind if I ask what your father does?" Gary said, looking around the kitchen in awe.

"He's a lawyer," Allison said, pulling open the door of a refrigerator that was about the size of the elevator they'd just been in. There was also a huge gas oven like the kind restaurants had, plus a microwave oven, plus about a hundred pots and pans and other utensils hanging on the walls.

"He must be a pretty good lawyer," Gary observed.

"Well, actually, he's a partner in his own firm," Allison said. "Ollquist, Sloan, and Barnes. Have you ever heard of them?"

"No. The only firm I've heard of is Dewey, Cheathem, and Howe," Gary said.

Allison bit her lip and giggled. "My father would love that one," she said, looking into the freezer compartment. "Do you like ice cream?"

"Love it," Gary said.

"What flavor?" Allison asked.

"What flavor do you have?"

Allison took a deep breath. "You better come look for yourself," she said.

Gary looked over her shoulder into the freezer. It was unbelievable—half a dozen carefully arranged rows of Häagen-Dazs in just about every flavor you could think of, two or three containers of each flavor stacked on top of each other in alphabetical order. Butter almond, chocolate, chocolate almond, chocolate chocolate chip, coffee . . .

"It's like being in a store," Gary said.

"That's my mother for you," Allison said.

Gary looked around the kitchen again. There was something else he hadn't noticed before. Everything was in perfect order. Pots on the walls were arranged from smallest to largest. All utensils were lined up according to size. Odds and ends on the counter weren't simply placed there. They were arranged neatly, by size or color or shape.

"She's a little bit compulsive," Allison said.

Gary nodded.

"So what flavor do you want?"

"Chocolate chocolate chip," Gary said.

Allison took out a container. Then she took a bowl out of a cabinet. "Would you like some cookies?"

Gary said he would and watched as Allison opened yet another cabinet. This one was filled with neat rows of Pepperidge Farm cookies. Again they were in alphabetical order. Gary chose chocolate-chip cookies.

"Chocolate chocolate-chip ice cream and chocolate-chip cookies?" Allison asked.

"I have a thing about chocolate," Gary said.

Allison brought all the food to the table. She gave him a good-sized bowl full of ice cream but took only a small cup for herself. The cookies were on a plate on the table between them.

"How come your mom puts everything in alphabetical order?" Gary asked as he scooped up some ice cream with a spoon.

"That's just the way she is," Allison said. "Sometimes I think that if my parents ever have another kid, its name will start with B and the one after that with C."

"You don't have any brothers or sisters?" Gary asked.

Allison shook her head.

"What's it like being an only child?"

Allison thought for a moment and then said, "I bet it's

sort of like being a rock-and-roll star with a fan club that has only two people in it. Your mother and your father."

"That sounds pretty good," Gary said, biting into a cookie.

"It is, as long as you always do what your fan club wants you to do," Allison said. "The second you try to do anything different, it's murder."

"They're strict, huh?"

Allison toyed with her spoon. "I'm not sure strict is the right word. It's more like they smother me sometimes. They let me stay out late, but the next day they want to know what I did every minute the night before."

"Can't you tell them to lay off?" Gary asked, thinking of his own mother.

Allison smiled. "I'm not sure that would go over well."

"What could they do?" Gary asked.

"They could send me to a private all-girls military school somewhere in Nebraska, I suppose," Allison said.

"Just because you told them to lay off?" Gary asked incredulously.

"Oh, I guess I'd have to do something worse than that," Allison said.

Gary shook his head in wonder. "I must tell my mother to get off my back at least once a day."

Allison seemed interested. "What does she do when you say that?"

Gary shrugged. "She just ignores me and keeps nagging."

"About what?"

"About sleeping too late and being a musician and not going to college. She's convinced I'm going to wind up as a bum on some street corner somewhere begging for quarters."

"Do you think you will?"

"I hope not," Gary said. "But the thing is you never know what's going to happen in rock. You could spend your whole life trying to make it and never get anywhere. I guess what bothers everyone is that there's no guarantee, like there is if you decide to be a lawyer or a doctor. I mean, no matter how much of a fool you are, you can always get a job if you have a degree."

Allison nodded. "You should hear what my father says about some of the lawyers he has to work with."

"Yeah, there are probably just as many berserko lawyers out there as there are berserko rock-and-roll bands," Gary said. "But somehow it's only the bands that get the reputation for being drug addicts and self-destructing by the age of thirty."

"But a lot of them do, don't they?" Allison asked.

"Well, some do," Gary admitted. "But some bands last twenty years or more. Look at the Stones and the Who. Sure, they were into a lot of craziness, but the times were crazy and I admit it's a crazy business. But somehow those guys managed to make great music for a long time. That had to take a lot of work. The problem is that most people outside the business don't see the work. All they see is a bunch of long-haired, stoned-out guys who sleep all day and play music all night. That's because the media perpetuates that image. I mean, who would be interested in a bunch of musicians who lived in the suburbs, got up at seven, and caught a train to the studio and rehearsed all day in jackets and ties?"

Allison grinned and put her finger to her lips.

Gary realized he'd gotten kind of wound up. "I'm sorry," he said in a low voice. "You think I woke your old man?"

Allison shook her head. "You certainly get emotional on the subject." She seemed amused.

"Yeah, well . . ." Gary just shrugged. He looked up at the kitchen clock. It was getting pretty late but he didn't want to leave just yet. He looked back at Allison. There was something he needed to know first. She'd come to see him at the Lounge. They'd held hands. All evening he had felt them growing closer. But what did it mean? It was a question he wanted to ask, but it wasn't the kind of question you asked in words.

With his heart beating faster than a piston in a small foreign car, Gary got up, walked around the table, and kneeled next to Allison so that their faces were only a few inches apart. The only time he could remember feeling this nervous was the first time the band played in front of an audience.

Allison didn't look nervous, but Gary had a feeling she was. She only hid it better than he did. For a few moments they stayed motionless, just looking into each other's eyes. Gary could hear the whir of the refrigerator across the kitchen and the vague, distant hum of traffic in the city outside. He could smell the perfume Allison was wearing and knew he wanted to kiss her. He leaned forward until his lips touched hers.

Allison kissed back softly and Gary tried to be calm and smooth, but he had a feeling that if he were wired to a dozen light bulbs at that moment, they all would have been glowing brightly. The kiss ended and they looked at each other. Gary knew he wanted to kiss her again, so he did.

It seemed like they kissed for a long time. Gary wasn't sure how long, but when Allison stopped to put on some ChapStick he got the feeling that her lips might be getting sore. And anyway, it was late. Allison yawned and Gary felt sleepy too. It would have been nice if he didn't have to go back out into the cold, and instead could spend the night there at Allison's. Gary chuckled to himself. Fat chance, kiddo.

He backed away a little and they looked at each other. Sometimes very early in the morning the city would finally grow quiet. Then, even though he was still awake, he would begin to feel like he was in a dream. He felt that way now. Like he was in a dream in which he was a young rock-and-roll star sitting in this magnificent apartment with a beautiful girl. Except the apartment was his. And he'd been working all week with his band in some fabulous recording studio, cutting their tenth album. And as soon as the album came out they'd go on a nationwide tour, with tours of Europe and Japan to follow. Then they'd take a month off in Tahiti before going back to the studio to cut their eleventh album. And on and on and on.

It was a nice dream, he thought. If only it would come true. Meanwhile Allison yawned the second time.

Gary pushed himself up out of the chair. "I guess I better go," he said. Allison nodded.

She let him out of the apartment and stood with him in the foyer while he waited for the elevator. He put his arms around her. She felt slim in his hands—a dancer's body. Their lips touched, a dream kiss, their bodies barely pressing against each other.

Bang! The elevator door slapped open and the next thing he knew Mr. Green was glaring at them.

"Oh, Mr. Green," Allison said angrily, her hands pressed against her chest, trying to catch her breath. "You scared us."

Mr. Green opened the elevator gate in stony silence. Gary felt like someone had just shot a gun at him, but he managed to step into the elevator. Allison waved good-bye and then he was plummeting downward in the elevator. Out of the dreamworld and back to earth.

Fifteen

Knocking. Somewhere deep in his sleep, Gary heard it. _Clunk, clunk, clunk,_ against his door. Bad news, go away, let me sleep. _Clunk, clunk, clunk._ The knocking was persistent. His biological clock kept telling him it was much too early to wake up, but Gary felt himself gaining consciousness.

Clunk, clunk, clunk.

Gary slowly opened one tired eye. The clock by his bed was a blur. The dial gradually came into focus. Oh, no! It was 10:30 in the morning. He'd only gone to bed four and a half hours ago.

Clunk, clunk, clunk.

Gary pulled the pillow over his head and pressed it against his ears. Why didn't they let him sleep anymore? Didn't anyone have any respect? He needed his sleep just like anyone else. Why couldn't they leave him alone?

Clunk, Clunk, Clunk! "Gary?"

"Go away," Gary groaned.

Now he heard squeaking door hinges. Someone was opening his door. Gary peeked out from under the pillow. Something light blue was moving slowly in the doorway. The process of identification and recognition occurred slowly in Gary's mind. Light blue = dental smock = father. Gary pulled the pillow over his head again.

He heard whispering. "He's asleep," his father's voice said.

"It doesn't matter," his mother's voice replied.

"Can't this wait?"

"No."

Soft footsteps approached. With his head still under the pillow, Gary imagined black wing-tip shoes stepping on his favorite guitar. A voice said, "Gary?"

"What?" Gary groaned.

"Uh, we have to have a talk," his father said.

"Later, I'm sleeping," Gary moaned.

There was a pause. Then Dr. Specter said, "I think it has to be now."

"Go away," Gary groaned.

"Gary!" The voice of his mother shot across the room from his doorway. "Listen to your father. Don't be disrespectful."

"I'm not being disrespectful," Gary moaned. "I'm being asleep."

"If we can get this over quickly, you can go back to sleep," his father suggested.

Gary pulled the pillow up slightly and watched while his father looked for a place to sit. Dr. Specter was a short, round bald man who periodically grew and shaved off a mustache for reasons no one could figure out. In fact, there was very little about Dr. Specter that anyone could figure out. One thing was obvious, though, and that was that he believed that most domestic concerns—including the upbringing of his two sons—were someone else's problem. Thus his contributions in that area had always been rare and never voluntary. Both Gary and Thomas appreciated that.

Finally his father sat down on the corner of Gary's bed. "I'm afraid your mother wants me to have a man-to-man talk with you," he said.

Gary's line of sight left his father and traveled to the doorway, where he could see his mother peeking in. "Why doesn't she have a woman-to-man talk with me?" he asked.

Dr. Specter glanced at the doorway and then back at Gary. "She feels that you don't listen to her," he said.

"So why should she think I would listen to you?" Gary asked.

"Gary!" the voice from the doorway said sternly. "Don't be fresh."

Gary sighed and Dr. Specter turned to the door and said to his wife, "All right. Leave us alone now, I'll handle this."

The door closed, but Gary didn't hear any footsteps going back down the hall.

Dr. Specter looked down at his son. "Gary, why don't you take that pillow off your head," he said.

"Because if I keep the pillow over my head, maybe I won't wake up," Gary said. "Then I can pretend this is all a bad dream."

Dr. Specter considered that for a moment and then shrugged. Maybe he could pretend it was a bad dream too. "All right, Gary," he said. "Last night your mother and I had a long discussion about this music business and she pointed out some very serious problems that I hadn't realized before. Now we both agree that you have the right to do what you like with your life, but it is not fair for you to drag your cousin and brother along with you."

The pillow was suddenly off Gary's head. He sat up and stared at his father. "Who said I'm dragging anyone any-where?" he asked, rubbing the sleep out of his eyes. "Susan and Thomas both want to be in the band. No one's dragging them. We're a good band. We're gonna make it. Even Barney Star says we're dynamite."

The door opened again and his mother asked, "Who in the world is Barney Star?"

Dr. Specter quickly turned. "I thought you wanted me to handle this myself," he said.

The door closed again.

Dr. Specter turned back to his son. "Now, Gary, no one says you're consciously making Susan and Thomas follow you in this music crusade of yours. But you have to recognize that you do influence them. Do you think they'd be so involved in music if you weren't?"

"I don't know," Gary said. "All I know is that no one is forcing them to be in the band. They both want to be in it. You make it sound like I'm a heroin addict and I'm trying to get them hooked on it too."

The door opened a crack. "That's next," his mother said.

This time Dr. Specter turned angrily. "Will you stop interrupting!" he yelled.

The door shut with a slap.

Dr. Specter turned to his son again. "Gary, you have to realize how you influence other people. Your mother tells me that Thomas comes home at night reeking of cigarette smoke. He's doing poorly in school and goes about in some kind of leather jacket with chains on it. And she's very upset that Susan has decided not to go to college. You know, until Susan's parents return from Australia, she's your mother's responsibility."

"But I didn't tell Susan not to go to college," Gary said. "She decided that on her own. And as far as Thomas is concerned, what do you think? That I stick the cigarettes in his mouth for him? You think I select his wardrobe? I don't like that stuff any more than you do. But the kid's fourteen. You try to tell him what to do."

Dr. Specter shook his head. "I'd rather not. But let me ask you this. What's going to happen in a month or six months from now when this fad is over?"

"It's not a fad," Gary said. "How can you talk about the band that way when you've never even heard us? We happen to be a good, competent, serious band. We work really hard and we're going to stick together and work at it until we make it."

"Which means what?" his father asked.

"Which means getting an album contract and starting to tour around other cities playing concerts and getting on the radio and TV," Gary said.

"And you really think that will happen?"

"Listen, Dad," Gary said. "Barney Star is a hotshot manager who's seen a lot of bands and he thinks we can make it. Now, he should know. He's in the business. And he says he's going to help us get a contract and get big gigs. He wouldn't be saying that if he didn't think we were good."

Dr. Specter rubbed his chin and didn't say anything.

"You know, Dad," Gary said, "it's really not fair of you to make judgments about our band, considering that you and Mom have never even come to see us."

Dr. Specter nodded, still rubbing his chin.

"And listen, Dad?" Gary added. "I really haven't gotten enough sleep. I was out late last night. So would you mind if I went back to sleep?"

Dr. Specter stood up. "You go ahead and get your rest," he said, walking back toward the door.

Gary rolled over and closed his eyes. He heard the door open and shut and then his mother's voice out in the hall saying, "You call that a man-to-man conversation?"

"I think Gary made some legitimate points," Gary heard his father reply.

Hallelujah! Gary thought, and fell asleep.

Tap. Tap. Tap. Someone was at the door again, but this was a different-sounding knock. Much lighter and more considerate. Gary peeked at the clock: 2:20. At least he'd gotten another four hours of sleep. Four and a half and four made eight and a half hours all together. Not bad.

Tap. Tap. Tap. "Gary?" It was Susan.

"Yeah, come in."

Susan came in and sat on the same corner of the bed his father had sat on earlier. She was wearing a blue running suit and jogging sneakers and her hair was pulled in a ponytail. She also had a can of Coke, which Gary immediately reached for.

"So what happened last night?" his cousin asked.

Gary took a gulp of Coke. There was nothing like a good hit of sugar and caffeine first thing in the morning. "What are you talking about?"

"Don't play dumb, Gary," Susan said, taking the can back. "I know you didn't get home until at least four thirty this morning."

"Try five thirty," Gary said, and yawned.

"Ooo la-la."

"Ooo la-la nothing, we spent most of the time talking."

"*Most* of the time?"

"Yeah, most of the time." Then Gary grinned a little. "But not *all* of the time."

"Hmmmm." Susan's eyes widened.

"Hey, don't get any ideas," Gary said. "She's not that kind of girl."

"What kind of girl do you mean?" Susan asked playfully.

"Aw, come off it, Susan."

"So you think she really likes you?" his cousin asked.

"Hmm, yeah, I guess." He yawned again.

"You don't seem very excited," Susan said.

"Just wait till I wake up," Gary replied.

"Are you going to see her again tonight?" Susan asked.

Gary shook his head. "Don't think so."

"When are you going to see her?"

Gary thought about it for a moment. Actually, he really didn't know. "Soon, I hope."

"Don't let her get away," Susan said.

Gary scratched his head. "What is she, a fish?"

Susan smiled and sipped some more Coke.

Gary sat up, swung his legs over the side of the bed, and pulled his jeans on. "I better go brush my teeth," he said.

His cousin also got up. "I wasn't going to say anything," she said, following him down the hall. In the bathroom she sat on the side of the bathtub while Gary washed his face.

"You know, my mother thinks I persuaded you not to go to college this year," Gary said as he dried his face.

"So? She can think that if she wants," Susan said.

"Yeah, but with your parents still in Australia on that fellowship, she feels responsible for you," Gary explained.

"Well, I can't help that, Gary," Susan said. "My parents and I talked it over months ago."

"Was the band really the only reason you didn't go to college this year?" he asked.

"Mostly," his cousin said. "But I also think that college is just a way of extending your childhood for another four years, and I'm tired of being a child. I wanted to try something different for a while. I wanted to get a job and be grown up for a change."

Gary squeezed some toothpaste onto his brush. "What about all the guys you used to go out with all the time? You used to party a lot and stay out late. Now all of a sudden you've got a job, you hardly go out, you jog and stuff. What happened?"

Susan shrugged her shoulders. "I don't know. I just changed, I guess. One day I realized that ninety percent of the guys I dated I didn't even like. Going out with them was just another thing I thought I was supposed to do. Like going to college. I'm supposed to go to college. I'm supposed to go out with guys. . . . Well, forget it. I'll go to college when I decide I want to go to college. And the same goes for guys. When I meet one I like, I'll go out with him."

She looked up at Gary. "Why are we so full of questions all of a sudden?"

He spat out some toothpaste foam and rinsed his mouth. "I don't know, Sue," he said, pulling his lip back and looking at his teeth. "I guess I've been wondering about all this stuff. It's like, you get out of high school and *bang!* Welcome to the real world. Everything gets serious all of a sudden. When we were in high school and we had a band, it was cool. But then, when you graduate and you tell people you're going to stick with the band instead of going to college, they look at you like you're crazy. Like it's not cool anymore. Now it's some kind of monster mistake that's gonna screw up your life forever. And I don't know. Maybe they're right. I mean, I don't want to be sitting in this house ten years from now wondering when my band is gonna make it and listening to my mother yell at me every day."

"Are you worried that Allison wouldn't want that either?" Susan asked.

"Well, Allison's part of it," Gary admitted. "I mean, how would you feel about going out with some guy who's living at home in a rock-and-roll fantasy while the rest of the guys his age had jobs or were in college?"

"You should give her more credit than that, Gary," Susan said. "She's not one of these little girls who throw themselves at you at gigs. I'm sure she understands how hard it is."

Gary nodded. "Yeah, but still. You should see where she lives," he said. "There are these limousines pulling up and people getting in and out. I mean, it makes me feel like I should be able to take her out and buy her more than a slice of pizza."

"You could always go to work in an ice cream shop," Susan said.

Gary pondered that. "On second thought," he said, "maybe she really likes pizza."

Sixteen

With Susan working in the Hole-in-the-Wall ice cream shop, it became the central hangout for the band. Not only was there free ice cream, hot chocolate, and soda, but the owners had installed a couple of video games as well. When Oscar and Karl weren't fighting over anything else, they were fighting over who was a better player.

"I did it! Six screens!" Karl yelled one afternoon. He was standing at the video machine wearing his Lenox Prep blazer and gray slacks. On closer inspection one would notice that he also wore a small gold hoop in his right ear.

Oscar turned away disgusted. "So big deal," he said. "Anyone can get six screens."

Karl remained hunched over the game controls, battling ionic spaceships, phaser monsters, and ultra lasers. In the midst of the action he said, "You've never even gotten five screens, Oscar."

"I haven't invested half of my life savings in that stupid

game, either," Oscar snorted, and headed for the table where Gary and Allison were sitting, sharing a free sundae.

"Anyone hear from Barney Star lately?" Oscar asked, sitting down.

Gary nodded toward Karl, who was still hunched over the controls of the video game. "Karl's our contact with Star. You better ask him when he's finished."

Oscar next looked at Susan, who was standing behind the counter in her candy cane outfit. "Can I have a hot chocolate?" he asked.

Susan nodded. "One free hot chocolate coming up." A moment later she handed him a steaming paper cup.

"You know," Gary said, turning toward his cousin, "I've begun to notice that you lack true capitalistic instincts."

"What makes you say that?" Susan asked.

"Well, basically, I don't think I've ever seen you charge anyone for anything," Gary said.

Susan crossed her eyes and stuck a finger in her mouth. "Oh, is *that* what you're supposed to do?"

Now the door of the shop opened and Thomas came in. His black hair was slicked back on the sides and fell in a curl on his forehead. He was wearing a black leather jacket, black pants, and heavy black engineer's boots.

"Oh-oh, the Hell's Angel has arrived," Oscar cracked.

Thomas gave him a stony glare. Over the last few weeks, he'd been working hard to perfect that look. It was part of his new tough-guy image. He went up to the counter and said, "Gimme a Coke."

Susan shook her head. "Sorry, we don't serve your kind here."

Allison giggled and Thomas shot her the stony glare. "You guys think you're so cool," he sneered. Then he swaggered away from the counter, lit a cigarette, and sat down by himself near the window.

"What's with him?" Susan asked.

"He thinks he's James Dean," Allison said.

"Who?" Oscar asked.

"You have to start watching late night TV movies," Gary told him. "*Rebel Without a Cause. East of Eden.*"

Over at the video game, Karl muttered, "Damn," and turned away.

"What happened, Karl?" Allison asked.

The drummer flopped down in a chair next to the table, and stretched his long legs out. "Stupid burrowing laser nailed me. I didn't even see it coming."

"How tragic," Oscar said.

"So what have you heard from Barney lately?" Gary asked.

"Talked to him last night," Karl said. "He told me he'll have a definite answer from DeLux this weekend."

"Keep your fingers crossed, guys," Gary said. He picked up his spoon and dipped it into the sundae he was sharing with Allison. He'd discovered that she would never order a sundae for herself, even though it was free. But she always managed to eat a lot of the ice cream he ordered for himself.

Now she had one last spoonful and got up. "I have to go to class."

Gary glanced up at the clock on the wall. It seemed like she'd just gotten there a few minutes ago. But Allison was picking up her dance bag.

"You gonna come hear us this weekend?" Gary asked. The band had a two-night job in Brooklyn. Instead of answering, Allison glanced at the others at the table. Gary knew that meant that she wanted to speak to him in private. He got up.

"Where are you going?" Karl asked.

"We have to talk about something," Gary said.

Karl smiled and exchanged looks with the others at the table. Gary knew they were always amused when he and Allison went off by themselves to talk.

Allison said good-bye to everyone while Gary grabbed his jacket. Allison pulled on a heavy wool sweater and they went outside.

It was cold and windy and Allison had to catch her hair in her hands and tuck it under the back of her sweater to keep it out of her eyes. Gary zipped his jacket up.

"Will you be disappointed if I don't come to the show?" she asked.

"Uh, I guess not," Gary said, even though he knew immediately that he was. For the last couple of weeks, Allison had come to all their gigs. Except for a few minutes in the ice cream shop each afternoon, it was the only time they got to see each other.

"But why don't you want to come?" Gary asked.

"Because it's all the way out in Brooklyn," she said. "I guess you'll leave in the afternoon and you won't be back until three or four in the morning. It takes up the whole day."

Gary nodded. He could understand her point, but he still wished she'd come. Even though he tried to spend just about every free moment he could with her, it never seemed like enough. Allison still went to ballet class most afternoons and her parents wouldn't let her go out on weekday nights.

"So, uh, what're you going to do instead?" he asked.

"There's a party Saturday night," Allison said.

"Oh." Gary looked down at the sidewalk. He hated to admit it, but he got jealous when she went to parties and stuff without him. She was a pretty girl and there were a lot of guys at parties. He scuffed his boot against the curb.

"Gary?" Allison said. "I wish you could go with me to the party. There are so many people I'd like you to meet."

Gary just shrugged.

"My friends keep asking to meet you," Allison said. "They all want to know who this mysterious guy is that I spend all my time with. The other day Tina and I actually had a fight because she says I spend too much time with you and not enough with her. I'm afraid she's right, Gary. Except for school, I hardly ever see her anymore."

The wind made little swirls of old leaves and city grit at their feet, and Gary shoved his hands in his pockets. "She could come to the gig too," he said.

Allison shook her head. "It's not just her, it's my other friends. And I wouldn't even want her to go to one of those crowded noisy clubs. It would be so nice if you could come to a party at someone's house where you could sit and talk without having to shout over the music."

Gary looked down at the curb. The truth was, he hadn't been to a party in a long time, mostly because the band played on weekend nights. He wished he could go with Allison. But it wasn't like he could call in sick. Especially now when things weren't going real well. He felt himself growing angry. If it wasn't for the stupid band, he'd be able to go to the party and have a whole evening with Allison for once. Instead he was going to spend the weekend dragging back and forth to Brooklyn, working for peanuts, and getting nowhere. It just wasn't fair to work so hard and not get anywhere and miss a good party too.

Gary looked at Allison. Boy, she was pretty. There were probably a hundred other guys around just waiting for a chance to ask her out.

"I guess it must get boring," he said, "watching us do the same show weekend after weekend."

Instead of answering, Allison moved close to him and took his arm and held it tightly. Their faces were only inches away from each other. "Don't be like that, Gary. You know I love watching you perform; it's just that Friday and Saturday nights are the only times I'm allowed to stay out late and I do have other friends I'd like to be with too."

"Yeah." Gary couldn't hide his disappointment. "So I

guess I won't be seeing you this weekend," he said dejectedly.

Allison thought for a moment. Then she said, "Well, there is one other possibility. You could come to my house for Sunday dinner."

That caught Gary by surprise. "You mean, with your parents?"

"My friends aren't the only ones who are curious about you," Allison explained. "My mother keeps asking me who I'm on the phone with every night. I think she'd like to meet you too. If you could stand it."

Gary chuckled. "Oh, I guess I could."

"Okay, I'll tell her you're coming," Allison said. "Now I really have to go." They quickly kissed and Gary watched as she hurried away. Dinner with the folks, huh? It wasn't as tempting as the party, but what the hell. He turned and went back into the ice cream shop.

"Aw, wasn't that cute."

Gary turned and saw Thomas in his seat by the window. He had a nasty smile on his face.

"You mind telling me what your problem is?" Gary asked.

Thomas just shrugged and gave Gary his well-practiced stony glare.

"You know, just because you dress like a punk doesn't mean you have to act like such a turd," Gary told him.

"Aw, go stick it up your nose," Thomas snapped.

Gary felt his fists clench. If it had been anyone else besides his little brother, he would have murdered him.

Seventeen

On Sunday at the Ollquists' the perfect meal was served by a maid in a spotless white uniform. Gary couldn't believe it. Actually, Allison had apologized for the maid ahead of time, explaining that she was only "a Sunday servant" and that the rest of the week the family managed its meals on its own. But on Sundays Mrs. Ollquist didn't like to cook. This was her day of rest.

When Gary asked Allison what kept her mother so busy during the week that she needed to rest, Allison replied, "Shopping."

Allison's parents dressed for Sunday dinner like it was some kind of fancy occasion. Mrs. Ollquist, a tall, very attractive woman whose hair was the same color as Allison's, wore a navy blue dress and matching shoes. Mr. Ollquist wore a dark suit and tie. He was tall and husky in a solid, square-jawed kind of way and Gary would have bet he'd played football in college. When Allison introduced Gary to him, he squeezed Gary's hand so hard that for a moment Gary wasn't sure if he'd ever be able to play guitar again.

Allison had dressed up, too, in a red dress with a blue flower print, and a string of pearls and pearl earrings. Gary thought she looked really pretty, although he would have felt more comfortable if she'd just worn jeans and a sweater. As for his own attire, after much deliberation he had decided to wear his old navy blue Lenox Prep blazer, a pair of straight-leg cords and a green T-shirt with a picture of Jimi Hendrix on it.

He didn't exactly feel at ease as he sat at the dinner table with Mr. Ollquist to his right, Mrs. Ollquist to his left, and Allison across from him. Everything about the room and the people in it was too formal. Too perfect. There were fresh flowers in a vase on the table, and brand-new candles. The plates were a pale cream color, rimmed with gold, and they all matched, as did the two forks, two knives, and two spoons at every setting. It seemed more like a fancy restaurant than someone's house.

No sooner had they sat down at the dinner table than the maid entered the room carrying a tureen, and ladled soup into a bowl in front of each person. She reminded Gary so much of a waitress that he wondered if he should leave a tip at the end of the meal.

"I see you're wearing a Lenox Prep blazer," Mr. Ollquist said as he lifted a spoonful of steaming soup toward his lips. "Are you a student there?"

"Uh, no, I graduated last year," Gary said. Across the table Allison smiled at him reassuringly. Gary tried the soup. It tasted good, but he had no idea what it was.

"Oh, then you're in college," Mrs. Ollquist said.

"Uh, no," Gary said.

One of Mr. Ollquist's eyebrows rose. "You're not in college?"

"Uh, no," Gary said again. He sipped another spoonful of soup and concentrated on not making any slurping noises.

"You're doing some sort of alternative study?" Mrs. Ollquist asked.

Gary shook his head. The dinner conversation was getting to be like a game of twenty questions.

"Gary is a musician," Allison said. "A very hard-working, dedicated musician."

"Oh." Mrs. Ollquist brightened considerably. "What instrument do you play, Gary?"

"Guitar," Gary said.

"Classical?" Mr. Ollquist asked.

"Rock," Gary answered.

There was another pause while this sank in. All Gary heard was the clinking of soup spoons against soup bowls.

"Do you mean," Mrs. Ollquist said, "rock as in rock and roll?"

"Yes." Gary nodded.

Mr. Ollquist cleared his throat. "I see," he said, as if something had suddenly become clear to him.

"Gary has one of the best bands in New York," Allison said. Her mother and father both nodded, but Gary had the feeling that he might have had the best car theft ring in the city, too, and it would have meant about the same to them.

The soup plates were now removed and dinner plates were placed before them. The woman in white came around with a silver platter and served each of them a slice of roast beef. Cooked carrots and peas were also placed on each plate.

For the moment, no one seemed to know what to say. Gary had the feeling that Allison's parents weren't sure what to do about this rock-and-roll musician sitting at their table. They probably had the same ideas about musicians that his mother had.

"You know," Gary said, "I think that people have a misconception about rock-and-roll bands. They still have this idea that we're maniacs and drug addicts, but it's not true anymore. The ones who are successful are hard-working people. It's a tough business and if you're going to make it, you really have to persevere."

Mr. Ollquist suddenly stopped in the middle of cutting his roast beef and gazed firmly at him, as if tempted to give Gary a lecture on the true meaning of perseverance. Fortunately, he seemed to decide against it and went back to his roast beef.

Mrs. Ollquist wanted to investigate further. "Tell me, Gary," she said, "do you perform regularly?"

Gary nodded. "Almost every weekend. And we also have rehearsals during the week."

"Where do you perform?" Allison's mother asked.

"At clubs," Gary answered. For some reason he was having a hard time cutting into his roast beef.

"Clubs?" Mrs. Ollquist echoed, apparently unsure of what Gary meant.

"Yeah, like rock clubs," Gary said, still trying to slice the meat.

"Oh," Mrs. Ollquist said as if she suddenly understood. "You're a nightclub entertainer."

"Sort of," Gary said. He realized that Mr. and Mrs. Ollquist had to translate what he did into something they could understand. And the closest thing in their world to what he did was a nightclub act. Gary didn't try to argue. He tried to cut his roast beef instead. He pressed down harder with the knife. Suddenly the roast beef slipped and hit the mound of green peas on the side of the plate, sending them sailing across the sparkling white tablecloth. Allison started to giggle.

"Oh, uh, I'm sorry," Gary mumbled, his face ablaze with embarrassment. He started to pick up the errant peas.

"Don't," Mrs. Ollquist said. She picked up a small glass

bell on the table and rang it. A moment later the maid appeared and, without having to be told, started cleaning up the peas. Gary was so embarrassed, he wanted to crawl under the table and hide.

"You had your knife upside down," Allison said, and bit her lip to suppress another giggle.

Gary looked at his knife. It sort of looked the same on both sides, but he realized she was right.

Allison turned to her parents. "Gary's band is trying to get a record contract. Everyone thinks they'll get one because they're so good."

Mr. Ollquist nodded and lifted a forkful of peas into his mouth. Then he dabbed a cloth napkin gently against his lips. "A fellow I knew at law school went into the record business," he said. "He's done rather well for himself."

"What company is he with?" Gary asked.

Mr. Ollquist turned and gazed at Gary, a slight smile on his lips. "I think the name is Multigram."

"I know them," Gary said, recalling his visit to Rick Jones. "I guess your friend is in the legal division or something, huh?"

"Well, not exactly," Mr. Ollquist said. "He's the president of the company."

After dinner Gary and Allison went into a living room filled with overstuffed furniture and lined with bookcases. Allison turned on some lamps and then sat down on the couch. Gary sank about a foot into the soft upholstery next to her.

"I can't believe what a jerk I made of myself," he said.

"Why, Gary?" Allison asked.

Gary turned back toward the dining room. He could see through the doorway to the dinner table, where Mr. Ollquist sat puffing on a cigar and talking to Allison's mother.

"Because I spilled peas all over the place," he said. "And

then I made that brilliant remark about your father's friend working for Multigram. I mean, the guy's the president of the stupid company."

"They know you didn't know," Allison said. She moved close to him and pushed some of the hair off his forehead with her fingers. Gary wanted to kiss her. But with Allison's parents right in the next room, he figured it wouldn't be such a great idea.

"Can't we go someplace more private?" he asked in a low voice. "Like your room or something?"

Allison shook her head. "I'm not allowed to have men in my room," she whispered back.

Gary was surprised. "Even with your parents home?"

Allison shook her head again. It was hard for Gary to believe. He could have people in his room any time he wanted, even all night long if he felt like it.

"I thought you said they trust you," Gary said.

"They do, but having a man in my room isn't a matter of trust," Allison said. "They think it's improper."

"Doesn't that bother you?" Gary asked. "I mean, them always telling you what's proper and improper?"

Allison shrugged. "Oh, I guess it does. But not enough to have a big fight about it. I save the big fights for more important issues."

"Like having a rock musician for a boyfriend?" Gary asked.

Allison chuckled and touched him lightly on the arm. "Don't worry about my parents," she said in a low voice. "They just take some getting used to."

Gary would have laughed out loud if Allison's parents hadn't been in the next room. "I think it's gonna be a lot easier for me to get used to them than it will be for them to get used to me."

"Well, that's their problem," Allison whispered, squeezing Gary's hand.

Gary nodded, but he couldn't help thinking that it was

really his problem too. "Let me ask you something else," he said. "If they think it's improper for you to have a boy in your room, does that mean it's also improper for you to be in a boy's room?"

"Oh, definitely," Allison replied. Then she smiled. "But what makes you think I'd tell them?"

Eighteen

As Gary walked home that night, a strong, cold wind whipped down the street, blowing dirt into his eyes. But all he could think about was Allison. The way he felt about her was amazing . . . almost frightening. She had brains, personality, warmth—everything. Up to now, music had been the most important part of his life, but sometimes when he was with Allison he didn't even care about it. All he wanted to do was run away with her to some place where there'd be no hassles with music, no hassles with parents, no hassles with life in general.

The wind was really stinging. Gary pulled his collar up around his neck and clenched his teeth in the cold. Too bad it was just a dream. There was no place to go and Allison probably wouldn't want to go anyway. And if he ran away from music now, he'd just be proving his mother and all the other doomsayers right. Besides, things were going to get better. Barney Star was going to get them a gig at DeLux.

He turned the corner and headed up the street where he

lived. Someone was sitting on the stoop of his parents' building with what looked like a backpack.

Damn, Gary thought, it was probably some bum who'd decided to make the Specters' stoop his home for the night. It wouldn't be the first time this had happened. Mrs. Specter always loved it when a bum sat on their front stoop. She never failed to remind Gary that he'd probably be sleeping on stoops someday, too, if he stayed in rock and roll.

But as Gary got closer, he noticed that the person sitting on the stoop had red hair and was wearing a familiar-looking Army surplus jacket. It was Karl.

"What's going on?" Gary asked.

Karl looked up with a crooked smile on his face. "Hey, Gary, you think I could stay here tonight?" He dragged deeply on a cigarette, and hunched over against the wind.

"Sure, but what happened?" Gary asked.

Karl exhaled smoke. "She found out," he said.

"Your mom?" Gary asked.

Karl nodded.

"About Star?"

"Yeah."

"And she threw you out?" Gary asked.

"Well, not exactly," Karl said. "I just kind of got the feeling that I wasn't totally welcome there anymore."

Gary sat down on the stoop next to Karl. The concrete step was cold and hard. "How'd she find out?" he asked.

"Well, from what I can figure, Star must have called DeLux and left a message for them to call back. Except when DeLux saw the name of our band, they called my mother, since she's still our manager. Someone at the club must have told her about Star."

Gary whistled.

"Anyway," Karl said, "while that was going on I was in the living room, working out on these practice pads I have for my drum set, right? Suddenly I looked up and there was this madwoman standing over me, and she looked like she was gonna kill me if I didn't tell her the whole truth and nothing but the truth. So I told her."

"So now she knows about Star," Gary said.

"Yeah."

Gary shoved his hands in his pockets. "I guess we just lost one of our managers, huh?"

Karl nodded quietly and lit a new cigarette off the butt of the old one.

"What did she say?" Gary asked.

"Not much," Karl said. "Actually, she said a lot, but it was sort of difficult to understand."

"Why?" Gary asked.

"Well, she was kind of pissed. I mean, she was definitely pissed. In fact, I think that for a while there she was temporarily insane."

The wind blew Gary's hair into his eyes and he pushed it away. "What did she do?" he asked.

"Well, first she just started screaming at me," Karl said. "I guess she figured out that we'd asked Star to work for us behind her back. But then, when she figured out that that was why we told her we wanted to take time off to work on new material . . . then she really went berserk."

"Why?" Gary asked.

"Because that's when she realized that we'd lied to her," Karl said. "She kept yelling about all the work she'd done for us and this is how we wind up treating her."

Gary nodded. The truth was they'd treated Mrs. Roesch pretty miserably and she'd never done anything to deserve it.

A cold gust of wind swirled around them and Karl shivered. Gary had no idea how long he'd been sitting out there on the stoop.

"You want to go inside?" Gary asked.

Karl nodded and picked up his pack.

The path from the front door up to Gary's room went past the dining room, and Gary knew there was no way he would be able to smuggle Karl past it without his parents' seeing them. They went down the hall and stopped in the dining room doorway. Inside, Gary's parents and Thomas and Susan were just finishing their Sunday dinner. They all looked surprised to see Karl.

Karl managed to smile a little and waved at Gary's parents. "Hi, Mrs. Specter, hi, Dr. Specter."

Gary's father waved back and said hello, but Gary's mother frowned when she saw him.

"Mom, do you think Karl could stay over tonight?" Gary asked. "He could stay in my room."

"Well, I suppose it's all right," Mrs. Specter said.

"Thanks, Mom," Gary said, and quickly pulled Karl toward his room before his mother could ask any questions.

It wasn't long before they were joined by Susan and Thomas.

Karl was sitting by Gary's window, smoking a cigarette and blowing the smoke into the air conditioning vent. When Thomas saw him, he said, "Hey, Karl, can I bum a smoke?"

"No," Gary snapped before Karl could answer.

"Why not?" Thomas asked.

"Because I don't want you smoking in my room," Gary said.

"How come it's okay for Karl and not for me?" Thomas wanted to know.

Gary wasn't in the mood to argue with his little brother. Things were bad enough at the moment without Thomas having to add to the hassles. "Look, why don't you just leave us alone," Gary told his brother.

"Aw, go screw yourself!" Thomas yelled at him. "You can pack your own van from now on." Then he slammed the door behind him.

"Gary, what's wrong?" Susan asked.

Since Karl didn't feel much like talking, Gary filled her in on the story.

When he had finished, Susan looked pretty somber. "So what happens now?" she asked.

Gary glanced toward Karl. "I guess this makes it really important that things with Barney Star work out," he said.

"Don't worry," Karl said. "They will. I'm sure of it."

Gary and Karl stayed up late that night, playing records and talking. Karl spent most of the time sitting near the air conditioner, chain-smoking cigarettes. He kept saying how great it was going to be once Barney Star got them a record contract. Gary tried to remind him that there were no assurances that they were going to get a contract. But Karl was convinced they would.

"I'm telling you, man," Karl said, "I know he's gonna come through. Don't you think our band is good enough?"

"Of course I think we're good enough," Gary said. "But I just don't know about Star. So far, he's been all talk. I haven't seen him produce anything yet."

"Give him a chance, man," Karl said.

Gary sat back. Karl was right. It was too soon to judge Star. They'd have to wait and see. It was just hard to sit around waiting when you weren't sure what you were waiting for.

"Hey, Karl," he said. "You think that Rick Jones guy at Multigram ever listened to our single?"

"Who cares?"

"I don't know," Gary said. "I guess sometimes this business really makes me sick. You try and you try. You call people and they never call back. You drop demos off and they never listen to them. Doesn't that ever get to you?"

"Yeah," Karl said. "But every time it does I just think about what it's gonna be like on our first big tour. Crowds of people digging our music everywhere we go. People dancing in the aisles, clapping and whistling, really into it. It makes all the hassles a lot easier to take."

"You really think that's gonna happen, huh?" Gary said.

"I'd be crazy to go through all this crap if I didn't," Karl told him.

Gary knew he was right. You had to believe in the big dream and the magic rock-and-roll fairy. Otherwise there was no point in it. The money wasn't that good, especially when you figured in all the hours of practice and rehearsals and all the equipment you had to buy. The working conditions were pretty poor and the hours were lousy. So it all came down to two questions. Did you believe? And were you willing to stake a year, or five, or even ten to find out if you were right?

Nineteen

The next morning Gary had a hazy recollection of Karl getting up early and dressing to go to school. Gary slept late, but even after he woke up, he still didn't want to get out of bed. He knew that his mother would be downstairs in the kitchen, planning a full-scale interrogation on why Karl had slept over.

The problem was, not only did he know that she was downstairs waiting, but she knew he was upstairs stalling. There was no escape unless he wanted to climb out his window and shinny down the drainpipe three stories to the ground. Gary looked toward the window. It was a tempting thought. Except that at some point he would have to come home and she would still be there.

So he had no choice.

Gary went downstairs. His mother was sitting at the kitchen counter, sipping a cup of coffee. She was wearing an old robe and her hair was pinned up, which meant she wasn't planning to go out soon. Gary paused in the doorway, his stomach rumbling hungrily, and then headed for the refrigerator.

His mother didn't even look at him as he crossed the kitchen and opened the refrigerator. She said nothing as he took out a Sara Lee coffee cake and the pitcher of orange juice, and ignored him as he cut a piece of cake and put it on a plate and poured some juice into a glass. As Gary put the rest of the cake and the pitcher back into the refrigerator, he began to wonder if he could actually escape uninterrogated. It was worth a try. He picked up the glass and plate, glanced at his mother one last time, and started toward the door.

"Gary?"

"Yeah, Mom?" Gary said, stopping short.

"Are you trying to avoid me?" his mother asked.

"No, Mom," Gary said. Reluctantly, he put the plate and glass on the kitchen counter and sat down on a stool across from her. "It's just that it's a real long story and I—"

"I already know the story," Mrs. Specter said, taking a sip of her coffee.

"You do?" Gary asked.

"Yes, Karl told me this morning," his mother said.

Gary took a bite of coffee cake. "He did?"

"Yes, dear," Mrs. Specter said. "And don't talk with food in your mouth."

Gary washed the cake down with some orange juice. "You saw him this morning?"

"I made breakfast for him," Mrs. Specter said.

Gary looked at his mother incredulously.

"It's a proven fact that children who have breakfast perform better in school than those who don't," Mrs. Specter said.

"Gee, Mom, thanks."

"Don't thank me," Mrs. Specter said. "I only did what any mother would do."

"So he told you?" Gary asked, biting off another piece of cake.

"Yes. It sounds very unfortunate," Mrs. Specter said. "It is obvious that the poor boy is very upset and doesn't know what to do."

"I guess," Gary said.

"So," Mrs. Specter continued. "I told him that he could stay here until everything is straightened out."

Gary almost fell off the stool. His mother had invited Karl to stay with them? Gary could only gape at her.

"Well, he doesn't have anyplace else to go, does he?" Gary's mother asked.

"Uh, well, no, I guess he doesn't," Gary managed to say.

"It's a wonder that in the midst of all this emotional tumult he can still manage to go to school," Mrs. Specter said. "It must be very important to him to continue his education. Which is more than I can say for someone else I know."

"He just wants to finish high school, Mom," Gary said.

"Well, I haven't spoken to him about college yet," Mrs. Specter said. "But if I can't talk any sense into you, I might as well try with him."

Gary finished his coffee cake and juice and took the empty plate and glass over to the sink. "Well, thanks for letting Karl stay here," he said as he left the kitchen. "I know he must really appreciate it. And so do I."

"If you really appreciated me," Mrs. Specter said, "you'd go to college."

Twenty

Barney Star wanted the band to meet him at a designer's studio on Seventh Avenue. He was formulating their "concept," he said, and it was going to require new performing outfits.

On the afternoon they were to go to the studio, Gary and Susan (who'd arranged to take off early from work) sat on the steps outside Lenox Prep and waited for Karl and Oscar. Gary was wearing his leather jacket and a scarf and sat with his hands jammed in his pockets. He was thinking about Allison. Because of this trip to the designer's studio, he wasn't going to get to see her that afternoon.

Susan was sitting on the steps near him, wearing a hooded sweat shirt and a denim jacket. "Thinking about Allison?" she asked.

Gary looked up. "How'd you know?"

Susan smiled. "It's easy. You have that distant look on your face. And anyway, you think about her all the time."

Gary felt his cheeks turn red.

A moment later the doors of the school opened and kids started pouring out. Karl and Oscar soon appeared, their school ties pulled loose and books under their arms. No sooner had Karl set foot outside the school than he dropped his books and lit a cigarette.

As the others watched, he took a deep drag and exhaled. "Ah, relief!"

Oscar joined Susan and Gary. "Life is one long nicotine fit for him," he said.

Karl picked up his books again, the cigarette hanging from the corner of his mouth. "Come on, let's go get a bus."

On the street in front of the school, they jumped on a downtown bus and sat down at the back. As it rattled and bounced down the city streets, Karl laid his schoolbooks flat on his lap and used them as a little platform to roll a joint. Gary noticed that a number of other passengers in the back of the bus were watching Karl with a mixture of curiosity and disapproval as he tapped some grass from a plastic pill bottle onto a piece of rolling paper.

"Uh, Karl," Gary said. "Is it really necessary to do that in front of all these people?"

Karl shrugged. "Nobody cares."

"Now, now, Gary," Oscar said. "You know Karl doesn't feel right until he's had his after school cigarette *and* his after school joint."

"Hardy har har," Karl grumbled.

The bus lurched along and Oscar turned to Susan. "So tell me, dear, how is life at calorie central?"

"To tell you the truth, Oscar, it's not as much fun as it used to be," Susan said. "Whoever promised me that I'd get tired of eating ice cream after the first week was lying. I think I've gained ten pounds since I started there."

Across from them, Gary half listened. He was still thinking about Allison and how much he hated not seeing her even one day.

Karl finished rolling his joint and looked up. "Hey, I think this is our stop."

They got off the bus. As soon as they were on the street, Karl lit the joint and took a deep toke. Meanwhile, the rest of the band checked out the area. Seventh Avenue was jammed with trucks and cabs. The sidewalks were crowded with men in work clothes pulling racks of dresses, and groups of fashionably dressed women and men going in and out of the tall buildings that lined the avenue.

"You know, this could be interesting," Susan said as she looked into a display window.

Karl took another toke off the joint and pulled a piece of paper out of his pocket. "It's that building," he said, pointing to a tall gray office building across the street.

The band weaved their way through the jammed traffic to the other side of the street and waited outside the building while Karl finished his joint.

"Is there anything else you'd care to smoke before we go in?" Oscar asked when Karl had finished.

"Very funny," Karl replied.

Inside the building they checked the names on a big directory board near the elevators: Calvin Klein, Halston, Perry Ellis, Sonia Rykiel . . .

"Uh, there it is," Karl said, pointing up at the board.

"Which one?" Susan asked, excitedly.

"Weinburger," Karl said.

"Weinburger?"

"Yeah, Murray Weinburger Limited. Ninth floor," Karl said.

"Not exactly what I had in mind," Susan said glumly as they got into an elevator and went up. When the doors opened they found themselves in an enormous low-ceilinged room filled with what must have been a hundred people, mostly women, sitting at sewing machines. There was a huge racket of sewing machines whirring and clacking and banging all at once. And all over the place, on the walls, on the floor, literally hanging from the ceiling, were thousands of scraps of fabric. It seemed as if they'd stepped into a wild forest of vines made of scraps and thread.

In one corner was a small office with big glass windows and inside they saw Barney Star slouched in a chair, smoking one of his thin cigars. Now he saw them and pushed open the door. "Hey, good to see you," he said, waving them in. "Murray just went to talk to someone. He'll be right back."

Gary and the band went into the office. There was an old wooden desk covered with a huge pile of disorganized papers and an old beat-up brown couch and chairs. Everything in the office looked ancient—the phone, the typewriter, the file cabinets all looked as if they'd been there since the turn of the century.

Barney invited them to take seats and then he sat down on the edge of the desk. He looked at them with his big magnified frog eyes and slapped his hands together. "So what's happening? How's it going?"

"Uh, not so great," Gary told him.

"Why not?" Barney asked.

"Karl's mother found out you were trying to book us at DeLux. She's really pissed."

Barney puffed on his cigar thoughtfully. "Hey, I'm sorry to hear that, man. But look, you guys weren't gonna last that long with her anyway, right?"

Gary shrugged. "I guess not."

"I mean, I'm trying to make things happen for you guys so you'll come with me, right?"

"So what have you made happen?" Susan asked.

Barney blinked and then said, "A lot. The possibilities are endless."

Susan glanced over at Gary with raised, doubtful eyebrows.

"What happened with DeLux?" Karl asked.

Barney waved the question away and took a silver case out of his jacket and offered his thin cigars. "Anyone care for one?"

"Uh, sure," Karl said.

Barney gave him one and lit it with a gold cigarette lighter. Meanwhile, Oscar muttered, "Karl, is there anything you won't smoke?"

"Look, will you get off my case already?" Karl said irritably.

"I'd really like to know what happened with DeLux," Susan said.

Barney paused and took a deep breath. "Well, uh, I didn't like their terms."

"What were their terms?" Gary asked.

"Uh, actually there were no terms," Barney admitted sheepishly. "Those guys are a bunch of little shots who think they're big shots. But you don't need them. I'm telling you, you'll do better with a showcase."

"A showcase?" Karl said.

"We put on our own show," Barney told them. "We rent out a club for the night and invite only the people we want to have there. We make a big deal out of it. Publicity, catering, by invitation only, the works. Selected members of the press are invited. A heavy dose of industry people. We make a big bang, wow the big shots, and the contracts start rolling in."

Gary had to admit that it sounded interesting. "You mean it's like a private audition for the music industry," he said.

Barney nodded. "Yeah, exactly."

"But how do we know they'll come?" Karl asked. "We've never been able to get them to come to our gigs before."

"Hey, you never had me for a manager before, right?" Barney said. "I'll tell you how we get them to come. We make them feel like if they don't come they're going to be missing something big. Nobody likes to be the only one left out, right? If they know everyone else is going, then they have to go too. We'll make this gig so hot that even a death in the family won't keep 'em away."

"Hey, that sounds pretty good," Karl said, smiling.

"In your condition, anything would sound pretty good," Oscar mumbled.

Before they could discuss it any further, an old man stepped into the office. He was almost completely bald with only a thin white fringe of hair going around the back of his head from ear to ear. He wore thick bifocal glasses and a long gray apron with scissors and measuring tape and pins sticking out of the pockets. Gary suddenly understood why everything in the office looked so old. This guy had probably been there since the beginning of time too.

Barney Star jumped off the desk. "Murray, this is my band. They're great, Murray. They're going to be big stars."

The old man smiled. He didn't have a lot of teeth. He went over to the band and looked at them. "They look like good kids, Barney," he said. "Are you good kids?" He reminded Gary of his grandfather.

"Uh, sure."

"You know I gave Barney his first job," Murray told them. "He was so green he didn't know a marker from a parka. He was a good boy. He worked hard for me. He was a good salesman, a natural. That's the best kind."

The members of the band glanced at each other, not sure what to make of this old guy or what he was telling them. Murray glanced back at Barney. "But then he got bit by the show business bug. Bit him right on the ass, if you'll excuse my language. And that was it. Forget the dress business. Now everybody's going to be a star." He pointed a gnarled, bony finger at the band. "You'll be stars. He'll be a star. I'd be a star, too, but I'll probably be dead first."

Barney seemed to be blushing. "Enough, Murray," he said, patting the old man on the back. "Let's get down to business. These kids don't care about ancient history."

Murray turned toward the door and called in a short, round woman, who took the measurements of each member of the band. While she worked, Barney told them how great the showcase was going to be. Gary was starting to wish that he'd save his breath.

Twenty-one

"Why am I starting to get this sinking feeling?" Gary asked later as he and Susan and Karl walked uptown looking for a pizza parlor. Oscar had gone home for dinner.

"Uh, because you're standing in wet cement?" Karl said.

"It's not funny, Karl," Susan said.

"I mean, the guy used to be a dress salesman," Gary said.

"I loved that line about not liking the terms from DeLux," Susan added.

"Hey, come on," Karl said. "Just because the guy was once a dress salesman and he couldn't get us into DeLux doesn't mean anything. I think this showcase idea sounds pretty good. Let's give the guy a chance, okay?"

"We don't have any choice, Karl," Gary said. "Your mother is through with us. Barney's the only thing we've got left."

"Not exactly a reassuring thought." Susan sighed.

They found a pizza place near 48th Street, where all the music shops were. Inside, they took a booth near the window and ordered some beer and a pizza with extra cheese and sausage.

"I just don't like it," Susan said. "I hate to be a downer, but I really think Barney Star is full of it. You can never get a straight answer out of him. We don't even know what other bands he manages. I say we get rid of him and try to get Mrs. Roesch back."

Karl shook his head. "No way. I called her yesterday." He sipped a beer. "She's still really pissed."

"Did you try to explain why we did it?" Susan asked. "Maybe if you told her that Oscar was threatening to quit and we thought it was the only way we could keep the band together. Maybe she'd begin to understand it a little more."

"She's still too mad to want to understand," Karl said.

A waiter brought a pizza and set it down on the table. They each pulled a slice onto a plate, and began to eat.

"You know what Star's initials stand for?" Susan asked.

"Barney Star," Karl said through a mouthful of pizza.

"Also BS," Gary said.

Karl shook his head and wiped his mouth with a napkin. "You guys are unbelievable. I mean, you're trying to convict Barney on circumstantial evidence. He used to be a salesman, one club said no, and his initials stand for a common slang expression and you think that's enough to send him to the electric chair."

Gary turned to Susan. "He does have a point, Sue. Stuff like what Barney used to do for a living really isn't any of our business."

But Susan disagreed. "I think it is our business. We're putting our band in his hands, Gary. What makes you think he's going to turn out to be any better than Mrs. Roesch? At this point I'd feel a lot better if we had someone I trusted managing us. Someone I really felt confidence in."

Gary was surprised. "I didn't know you felt that strongly about it."

"If you spent all day in that ice cream shop, you'd be a lot more interested in seeing our band make it too," his cousin said. "After you've worked for minimum wage for a month, you realize that there are a lot of worse things you can do than be in a successful rock band."

Karl nodded. "As a former bicycle messenger I can attest that she speaks the truth."

"Okay, look," Gary said. "I have no great love for Barney Star. But one of the things we're so pissed about is that none of the big clubs or record companies will give us a chance, right? So it would be pretty hypocritical if we didn't at least give Barney a chance."

Susan shrugged, but didn't reply, and for a few moments they concentrated on their pizza. As Gary pulled a new slice off the pie, he looked out the window and saw a tall guy with long blond hair standing on the sidewalk, looking in. He was wearing a long green Army surplus coat and carrying a guitar case.

"Hey, that's Johnny Fantasy," Gary said. Johnny was the lead guitarist of the Zoomies, the band Gary had always felt was the Coming Attractions' chief competition among the young, unsigned bands in New York. That was, until Oscar found that article in *Billboard* saying that the Zoomies had produced an album and were supposed to tour through fifteen states.

Gary waved and Johnny saw him and came into the pizza shop. Over the previous summer the two bands had played on enough double bills to become friendly rivals. Gary and the others made room for Johnny at their table and the tall guitarist sat down.

"Think I could bum a slice?" Johnny asked, staring at the pizza.

"Sure, go ahead," Gary said.

"So how's it going?" Karl asked as Johnny pulled a slice from the pie and bit into it hungrily.

Johnny shrugged. "Pretty crappy."

"But we read that you guys had an album contract and were going to tour for six weeks," Gary said. "It sounded great."

Johnny nodded and sprinkled some garlic powder on his pizza. "It sure did, man. Sounded unbelievable. The record company put us in the studio and promised us a tour and everything. The real star treatment. We cut the album, mixed it, did the cover art. It came out about three weeks ago and it was panned, man. I mean, those reviewers are ruthless."

"Aw, man, that stinks," Karl said.

"Well, it was just bad timing," Johnny said. "This month they don't like pop music. Next month maybe they'll love it. Anyway, as soon as the reviews started coming in, it was like freezeout city at the record company. No one was returning our phone calls. All of a sudden everyone was out of town, on vacation, or in an important meeting and couldn't be disturbed."

"Geez."

"Then the next thing we knew, there was no more tour," Johnny said. "They canceled it. We were gonna try and sue 'em for breach of contract, but forget it. It's all there in the fine print. They can cancel the tour if they want to. They don't even have to release the album."

"That's unbelievable!" Gary gasped.

But Johnny only shook his head. "No, man, that's the music business. When you're hot, they love you. But when you're not, they don't even remember your name."

"What are the Zoomies going to do now, Johnny?" Susan asked.

The guitarist shrugged. "Well, it's been a pretty heavy blow. A couple of the guys aren't sure they want to stay in the band. I can't really blame 'em. You can only bang your head against the wall for so long. Some of 'em are talking about going back to school or getting steady jobs."

"What about you?" Gary asked.

Johnny grinned. "I'll stay with it. You know, give lessons, do session work, commercials, whatever comes along. I mean, what else can I do? Playing guitar is the only thing I know. Eventually, I guess I'll try to put together another band and figure out what the next fad is gonna be."

Gary and the others nodded. Talk about disappointing news. Meanwhile, Johnny took another bite of pizza and asked what the Coming Attractions were up to. Gary told him about losing Mrs. Roesch and the showcase Barney Star was planning.

"You ever hear of Barney Star before?" Karl asked.

Johnny shook his head. "Naw, there are so many of these guys running around. You never know. Sometimes you get a good one, someone who really knows his stuff. But sometimes you wind up with some kook who just likes to hang out with rock bands and meet girls. Anyone can decide to be a rock manager. It's not like you need a diploma or anything."

Susan nodded knowingly.

"What do you think of the idea of a showcase?" Gary asked.

"Who knows, man? You try anything that sounds like it might work. If it does, great. If not, you gotta try something else. I'll tell you though. Things only have to blow up in your face a couple of times and you'll know pretty quick whether you're just in this scene for a fun time, or whether you're in it because you just can't be anyplace else. I can see why a lot of bands quit, and I can't say I blame them."

Gary sat back. It was hard to believe these words were coming from Johnny Fantasy. The guy had always been so gung ho about rock.

Johnny finished his slice and got up. "Hey, thanks for the pizza," he said. "I gotta split, but good luck with your showcase."

As he picked up his guitar case, Karl nodded at it. "You got a gig or something?"

Johnny cracked a smile. "No, I gotta get over to the music shop before it closes. This is one of my spare axes. I hate to do this, but I gotta sell it to pay the rent this month."

The band watched silently as Johnny left the pizza place and headed toward the music shops on 48th Street. There was still a slice of pizza left on the tray, but none of them had any appetite for it. Karl took a sip of beer and glanced at the others. "That," he said, "was depressing."

Twenty-two

The showcase was only a week away and the band was looking forward to it eagerly. They spent extra hours in the rehearsal studio sharpening their act and almost every night Susan and Karl and Gary would get together in Gary's room to work on new material. They wanted to do everything possible to make the showcase a success.

The addition of Karl to the Specter household was easier than Gary had expected. Mrs. Specter really did seem sympathetic and treated him like another son, and Karl said he appreciated her because she cooked real food instead of the frozen TV dinners he was used to getting at home. On the other hand, it was difficult to tell whether Gary's father understood that Karl was actually living with them. One night after dinner Dr. Specter waited until Karl had left the table and then turned to Gary and asked him why his friend was eating over so frequently.

"He's been living here for weeks, Dad," Gary said.

Gary's father gave him a blank look. "You mean, sleeping here?"

Gary nodded.

"Does your mother know?" Dr. Specter asked.

"Of course she knows, Dad."

Dr. Specter seemed to relax. As long as his wife knew, it wasn't his problem.

There was one other important event scheduled before the showcase. Allison's dance class was going to put on its first recital and Allison wanted Gary to come.

"I have just one question," Gary said.

"Yes, my parents will be there," Allison said, taking the words out of his mouth. "You know, they don't hate you."

"They just hate what I do," Gary said.

"No, I'm not sure they understand what you do," Allison told him.

"Great," Gary said. "Maybe I should teach a course. Introduction to Rock and Roll."

"Gary . . ."

"Okay, okay. You know I wouldn't miss it."

The recital was in the same room where Gary sometimes watched Allison practice after school. But this time a couple of dozen folding chairs had been placed in rows in the back and a table had been set up along one side with a punch bowl and cookies. As far as Gary could tell, the crowd gathering was mostly the parents and friends of the dancers. He looked around for Allison, but couldn't find her. She was probably in another room somewhere warming up for the recital.

There were still a few minutes before the program would begin, so Gary went over to the snack table. A young woman wearing a pink dress poured the punch for him and he picked up a couple of cookies. Then he turned around and practically walked into Mr. and Mrs. Ollquist.

"Why, Gary, hello," Mrs. Ollquist said, all smiles. She was wearing a blue dress and pearls. Beside her, Mr. Ollquist was wearing a dark gray pin-striped suit.

"Oh, hi, Mrs. Ollquist, Mr. Ollquist," Gary said, allowing his hand to be subjected to another bone-crushing handshake from Allison's father.

"Allison told us you might come," Mrs. Ollquist said. "Are you interested in ballet?"

"Well, uh, to tell you the truth, I don't know much about it," Gary said.

"Oh, there isn't really much you have to know," Mrs. Ollquist said. "It's simply beautiful to watch and enjoy." She turned to her husband. "Isn't that right, darling?"

"Oh, yes, of course," Mr. Ollquist said. He looked kind of bored, and Gary suspected he wasn't the world's greatest ballet fan.

"We were so glad when Allison took an interest in ballet," Mrs. Ollquist said. "When you think of some of the other things teenagers get involved with . . ."

Her words trailed off and Gary had a feeling he knew why. She'd probably just remembered that he was a rock-and-roll musician. Chances were that one of the "other things" she was glad Allison hadn't gotten involved with was rock and roll. Mrs. Ollquist looked embarrassed, but Gary decided to relieve her.

"I think," he said, "the great thing about ballet is that it combines art with exercise."

Mr. Ollquist glanced at Gary with a raised eyebrow.

He probably thinks I'm full of it, Gary thought, and he's right.

"I absolutely agree," Mrs. Ollquist said. "And I think it is also a wonderful form of discipline. But . . ." Mrs. Ollquist lowered her voice. "I do hope Allison doesn't decide to make a career of it."

"Why not?" Gary asked, honestly surprised.

"Because this ballet school costs an arm and a leg," Mr. Ollquist grumbled.

"Oh, it's not that," Mrs. Ollquist said, nudging her husband playfully on the arm. "But you hear about the lives of young ballerinas and it seems so . . . so rigorous. They hardly have time for anything except dancing."

"And buying clothes," Mr. Ollquist added.

Now the ballet instructor, the man the dancers called the bulge, stood in front of the room and asked everyone to be seated. Mrs. Ollquist asked Gary to join her and Mr. Ollquist and they sat down on the metal chairs.

The gray-haired pianist started playing, and eight ballerinas, including Allison, ran out of a door on the side of the room and took a position, stiffly holding their arms and legs. The bulge nodded and they went right into their dance. All the girls had their hair pulled back severely behind their heads into buns and they wore dark eye-shadow and lipstick. Allison was dancing on her toes, concentrating, never even glancing toward Gary or her parents. Gary thought she was the prettiest ballerina on the floor. He glanced at Mrs. Ollquist, who seemed enraptured as she watched her daughter. Next to her, Mr. Ollquist had folded his arms and closed his eyes. He was snoring.

Halfway through the performance there was a short intermission. The dancers disappeared through the door on the left side of the room, and most of the audience turned to chat with each other. Since Mr. Ollquist was pretty much asleep, Mrs. Ollquist turned to Gary.

"I'm afraid my husband can sleep through anything," she said, somewhat amused.

"Well, he probably works pretty hard," Gary said, trying to be polite.

"Oh, yes," Mrs. Ollquist said. She took a tissue from her bag and blew her nose gracefully. Gary wondered if she did anything ungracefully. "You know, what he said before about the lessons. He really is happy to pay for them. He, well, sometimes I think he feels obligated to be grumpy."

Gary smiled. "In my family, my mother has that role."

Mrs. Ollquist laughed lightly. Gary figured either she was just very polite or she was a lot nicer than he'd originally assumed. Maybe Allison was right about her parents. It just took a while to get to know them. He could already tell that he would like Allison's mother. Her father, though, was another story.

The intermission ended and Mr. Ollquist managed to snooze right through the rest of the recital. Gary had to admit that by the end he, too, was about ready to fall asleep. Of course, he kept himself awake and pretended to be interested. He noticed that as soon as the applause began, Mr. Ollquist not only woke up, but started applauding enthusiastically, as if he'd watched and enjoyed every moment.

When the performance ended, the dancers disappeared through the side door again. Mrs. Ollquist was talking to her husband, so Gary looked off in another direction. He saw two girls about Thomas's age several rows away, looking at him and whispering to each other. Now they got up and came over, kneeling on some empty seats in the row in front of Gary.

"Aren't you Tommy Specter's brother?" one with long blond hair asked.

Gary nodded. He noticed that Mr. and Mrs. Ollquist had stopped their conversation and were listening.

"You've got a great band," the other girl said. She had curly black hair and was chewing gum.

"Yeah, we want to come see you at a club, but our parents won't let us go alone," said the first girl.

"Then where'd you hear us?" Gary asked.

"We heard you at the Third Avenue fair last summer," the girl with black hair said.

Now the other girl pressed the dance recital program toward him. "Would you autograph it?" she asked.

"Uh." Gary patted his pockets. "I don't have a pen."

"Oh, I think I have one," Mrs. Ollquist said, digging through her bag. She found a pen and handed it to Gary, who signed the program.

"Are you going to play any more street fairs?" one of the girls asked.

"Maybe next summer," Gary said, handing the program back.

Both girls looked disappointed. "Oh, I don't want to wait that long," one said. "Don't you have an album or anything?"

Gary shook his head.

"How come?" the blond girl asked.

"It's hard to get an album contract," Gary said.

"But I hear albums all the time by bands that are totally lame compared to yours," said the girl with black hair.

Gary chuckled. "Thanks," he said. "Don't worry, we'll have an album one of these days."

The girls nodded and then the blond one asked, "Does Tommy have a girlfriend?"

"No, I think he's playing the field," Gary said.

"See, I told you," she said to the other. Then the two girls got up and headed for the refreshment table.

Gary realized he was still holding Mrs. Ollquist's pen. He handed it back to her. "Uh, thanks."

"Fans?" Mrs. Ollquist asked with an amused look on her face.

"I guess," Gary said.

Now the dancers came back out in their street clothes and the audience applauded them again. Allison came over and sat in one of the chairs Gary's groupies had just kneeled on. She'd let her hair out of the bun and had scrubbed all the makeup off, except for some eyeliner.

"I thought you were marvelous," Mrs. Ollquist said.

Allison looked at Gary. "What'd you think?" she asked.

"You're really good," Gary said.

"Oh, you're just saying that," Allison said. She turned back to her mother. "Did Dad manage to see any of it before he fell asleep?" she asked, teasingly.

Mr. Ollquist cleared his throat, but didn't say anything.

"If you have to snore," Allison told him, "at least try to snore in time to the music. It would be much less obvious that way."

Only a daughter could get away with that, Gary thought.

Since it was a school night, the chances of Allison being allowed to stay out after the recital were nil. But as they left the ballet school, Mr. and Mrs. Ollquist went ahead to let Allison and Gary have a moment in private.

"How were they?" Allison asked when her parents were out of earshot.

"Not bad," Gary said.

"See, I told you." Allison smiled.

"It's funny the way you tease your father," Gary said.

Allison laughed. "Oh, come on, Gary, he's just a big teddy bear."

"I believe you about the bear," Gary said. "It's the teddy part I'm not so sure about."

"Allison looked over at her parents. "They're waiting for me. I really have to go," she said hastily. "Is everything set for the showcase?"

"Yup. You sure you can't make it?"

Allison tilted her head toward her parents. "I wish I could, but not on a school night."

Gary nodded. "It's probably just as well. I'll be nervous enough as it is."

"Oh, I'm sure you'll be great," Allison said. Then she kissed him on the cheek. "Will you promise to call me afterward and tell me how it went?" she asked as she walked away.

"Sure." Gary waved and watched her join her parents. Geez, he really was a little nuts about her.

Twenty-three

On the day of the showcase, Gary was up early. He was too excited to stay in bed and there was too much to do anyway. The first thing he did was go downstairs to his father's office. It was the regular receptionist's day off and Mrs. Specter was filling in for her.

Gary came in through the back stairs. As usual, there were a couple of patients sitting around in the yellow Naugahyde chairs, reading magazines and waiting for Dr. Drill. Gary's mother was sitting behind the receptionist's desk.

Her jaw dropped when she saw him. "Gary, what's wrong? It isn't even noon yet. Can't you sleep?"

Gary chuckled. "Very funny, Mom. I came down to see if you and Dad wanted to come to the showcase tonight. I think it would be a good opportunity for you to hear us. And there won't be any drug-crazed maniacs running around either."

His mother was obviously surprised by the invitation. Gary had never really wanted her to see him perform before, but he thought that if she saw their act, maybe she wouldn't give him such a hard time.

"Well, thank you for asking," Mrs. Specter said. "Unfortunately, we're going to be busy tonight."

"You sure?" Gary asked.

"Maybe another time, dear," Mrs. Specter said. "But since you're down here, there is something else I want to talk to you about."

She stood up and Gary followed her down a hallway. Drilling sounds were coming from one room and as Gary passed it he caught a glimpse of his father and an assistant leaning over a patient. Gary cringed at the high-pitched whine of the drill. Farther down the hall, Mrs. Specter pushed open a door marked "Lab." There was a young woman in white inside taking instruments out of the sterilizer.

"Cathy," Mrs. Specter said. "Would you go out and cover the phones for a moment while I speak to Gary?"

Cathy nodded. As she went out, Gary winked and she said, "Hi, Gary," and giggled. All the girls in his father's office kidded around with him.

Mrs. Specter sat down on a stool. Gary leaned against a cabinet and glanced around at the grinding machines and sterilizers and the shelves where dozens of pairs of false teeth sat. Gary always imagined they were grinning at him.

His mother picked some lint off her outfit. "Mrs. Roesch called this morning," she said. "She's very upset and she wants Karl to come home."

"That's not what Karl says. He says she doesn't want him to come home."

His mother nodded. "She thinks he's saying that because he feels guilty about the way you've treated her, and he doesn't want to go home and face her."

Gary could understand that. He wasn't particularly keen on facing Mrs. Roesch himself.

"You know, Gary," his mother said. "Sometimes it's better to stand up and tell someone the truth instead of letting them find it out on their own. I'm not saying you should have kept Mrs. Roesch as your band's manager. But if you weren't going to use her anymore, you should have told her."

"Yeah," Gary said. He'd pretty much figured that out on his own. Now he gazed around the room at all the smiling false teeth and imagined that they were agreeing with his mother. "You're not gonna kick Karl out, are you?" he asked.

Mrs. Specter shook her head. "Karl will have to decide for himself when to go home. Of course, it might help if you talked to him about it."

"Maybe after the showcase tonight."

Mrs. Specter nodded and stood up. "I take it that this is going to be very important for your band."

"Probably the most important thing that's ever happened to us," Gary said. "This could really be our big break."

Mrs. Specter looked up at the ceiling and then back at her son. "Well, I hope it works out," she said.

Gary could hear the resignation in her voice. Could it be that she was finally beginning to understand how important music was to him? Was she really going to accept the idea that he had a life of his own? Gary refused to believe it. It was too good to be true.

Barney Star had picked a small, chic-looking club in Greenwich Village called the Lewd. It was beautifully decorated in art deco style with pink walls and a black tile dance floor. There were plush booths lined in velvet, and ornate lights and in the center of the room a caterer's table was covered with cold cuts and fruits and cheeses. A florist had been hired to do settings on the table and in front of the stage. Gary could see that Star had gone all the way; the results looked impressive.

Barney himself showed up in a suit and tie, with his cowboy boots well polished. He was as buoyant and as excited as a little kid at his birthday. After the band did their sound check, he gave them the outfits he'd had made for their performance.

"This is the kind of image you kids need," he said as he handed each of them a jump suit made of a different color of material. Oscar's was purple, Karl's was black, Susan's was hot pink, and Gary's was aqua blue. Stitched in bold red letters on the back of each was "Coming Attractions," as well as the musician's name on the front.

They went into the dressing room to put them on. The jump suits were new and stiff, but they fitted pretty well. When the band left the dressing room Barney clapped his hands together. "Great! You look like dynamite." Then he turned away to talk to the caterer.

The members of the band looked at each other.

"We look like designer garage mechanics," Oscar said.

"Cool it, Oscar," Gary whispered. "If this is what Barney thinks we need to get a contract, we do it."

So everything was set. Even Susan had to admit the club looked great. The food, the outfits, the flowers—all contributed to the classy look Barney wanted. Now all they had to do was wow the big shots.

But first the big shots had to come.

They waited. Up on the stage, Gary and the band nervously tuned their instruments. Behind the Lewd's bar, a bartender dried glasses and set them out in neat rows. Near the door, Barney Star paced back and forth, smoking a thin cigar and glancing at the club's entrance.

And waited. With their instruments tuned to perfection, the band had nothing to do except stand around. The bartender crossed his arms and leaned against a case filled with liquor bottles. Barney went outside.

And waited. Oscar sat on the edge of the stage. Gary and Susan sat on their amps. Behind the drum set, Karl lit a cigarette. A couple wearing matching black velvet baseball jackets came into the club and started eating the caterer's food. Gary had no idea who they were, but he didn't think they were music people. The same went for three preppy-looking guys who stopped at the bar and ordered drinks.

And waited. The couple in the baseball jackets left and Barney came back in, looking disappointed. Susan did some aerobic stretches. Oscar was sitting at one of the tables, reading a newspaper. The bartender had turned on a small television behind the bar.

At a quarter to eleven Barney called it quits. More than two hours had passed since the official "start" of the showcase. The band wasn't even on the stage anymore. They were just sitting around a table, stunned and disappointed. Mostly, they felt the silence. Barney walked up to the table. It seemed like he'd gone through an amazing transformation since early in the evening. He looked disheveled and beaten, like a doctor who'd been up for days trying to save a dying patient, only to fail in the end.

"I'm sorry," he said, puffing on the butt of a thin cigar. "You kids might as well pack up. No one's gonna come."

"What happened?" Susan asked.

Barney took off his glasses and rubbed the bridge of his nose. "I wish I could tell you, but I don't know. I really don't." His confidence was gone, there was no BS in his words. No one else seemed to have anything more to say, and Barney turned and walked slowly out of the club. Gary realized that he almost wished Barney had BSed them. Even a lame excuse was better than no excuse at all. It would have left them with at least a glimmer of hope. Now they had nothing.

Twenty-four

A light snow fell over the city the next afternoon, dusting the grimy streets and buildings like talcum powder. The wind blew swirls of snow down the sidewalks until it collected in cracks and crevices. Gary stood near the entrance to the Ripton School, his hands jammed in the pockets of his leather jacket and his ears tingling from the cold. Snow was getting into his hair. It hadn't occurred to him to wear a hat.

Every once in a while someone on the sidewalk or a student entering or leaving the school would pass and give him a peculiar look. After all, it wasn't the kind of day you spent just standing around outside. And it was much too early to be waiting for anyone to get out of school. The first students wouldn't start to leave Ripton for at least another hour.

But Gary didn't care. There was no place else to go and no one to see, except Allison. He didn't want to stay at home, he didn't want to go to the ice cream shop, and he definitely didn't want to see anyone else from the band. He just

wanted to be alone and wait. Besides, the snow and the cold
didn't bother him much. Except maybe for his ears and toes.
And for some reason which he couldn't explain, that was
okay.

"Gary?"

He turned and looked up the old marble steps to the front
of the school. Allison was holding one of the wooden doors
halfway open and looking down at him. She was wearing a
pink sweater and jeans. The wind caught her hair and
whipped it wildly.

"What are you doing?" she asked.

Gary shrugged. "Just waiting."

Allison studied him. "Want to come in?"

"Okay." Gary climbed the steps and went into the vestibule.

Allison closed the door behind him. "You're covered with
snow," she said, brushing the snow off his shoulders. "How
long were you out there?"

"Not that long," Gary said.

"Were you just going to wait until school was over?"

"I guess. I don't know. How'd you know I was out there?"

"Tina saw you through the window." She gave him a
concerned look. "Did something happen at the showcase?"

"It was a total flop. Five people showed up. It was a complete waste."

"Oh, Gary, I'm sorry," Allison said, putting her hand on
his arm.

Gary shrugged. "I'm not surprised. I was never totally
sure of Barney Star. I guess I should have trusted my instincts more."

Allison nodded. She crossed her arms tightly in front of her
and seemed to shiver. It was cold in the vestibule. They
were standing on a wet black rubber mat and drafts were
coming in.

"Can we go inside?" Gary asked, pointing at the second set of doors that led into the school corridors.

Allison shook her head. "You're not allowed. But we can stay here. What are you going to do about the band?"

Before Gary could answer, the bells rang and girls started pouring out of classrooms. A lot of them passed the vestibule and stared at Gary and Allison.

"Sort of makes you feel like you're in a cage at the zoo," Allison said, looking out.

"What about your next class?" Gary asked.

"Poetry seminar," Allison said. "I can be a little late. What did the rest of the band say?"

"I don't know." Gary looked down at the black mat and the dirty pools of water that had formed from melting snow. "I haven't talked to anyone since last night. I think we were all too bummed out to know what to say."

Allison looked sad. "Oh, Gary, I feel awful."

Gary watched the girls passing in the corridor, still staring at him and Allison. More than anything he wanted to pull her into his arms and feel her soft warm face against his cold wet skin. He looked back at Allison and knew that she felt the same way. She touched his hand.

"I have to go," she said. "Will you come over to my house after school."

"What about ballet?"

"I'll skip it."

"Your parents?"

"Mom went to visit her sister in Connecticut for a few days and Dad's been working late," Allison said.

Gary felt a small smile creep onto his face. Allison kissed him quickly on the cheek and went back into school.

That afternoon Gary finally got to see what Allison's bedroom looked like. It wasn't what he'd imagined. Allison always seemed so neat, but her room was . . . not exactly a pigsty, but close. Sweaters and jeans and ballet clothes were draped over chairs, chests, and bedposts. There was nothing dirty about the room, it was just that Allison didn't bother to hang things up or put them away after she wore them.

"This must drive your mother crazy," Gary said. He was lying with his head on her lap while she smoothed out his hair.

"Not anymore," Allison said. "It used to, but now she just pretends that this room doesn't exist. All she asks is that I keep the door closed."

"I hope it's not an offense punishable by sentencing to a private all-girls military school in Nebraska," Gary said.

"If it was, I'd clean it," Allison said. She ran her finger over his nose. It tickled. "What do you think you'll do now?" she asked.

Gary reached up and put his hands around her neck and pulled her face down toward him. "Kiss you," he said as his lips touched hers.

When the kiss was over, Allison straightened up again. "Thank God I'm limber," she said. "And you still haven't answered my question."

"I guess I have to see what everyone else wants to do," he said.

"But you're the leader. Don't you think that a lot of how they feel is going to depend on what you do?"

Gary shrugged. "I can't make them play."

"You can encourage them. You can say, 'The hell with Barney Star. Let's keep going.'"

Gary gazed up at Allison. "If we go back to gigs every Friday and Saturday night, I'll never get to see you."

"But if you don't go back, what will you do?"

He shrugged. "I don't know. Become a Zen Buddhist monk and transcend the material world. Or, maybe go to college and extend my adolescence another four years. Or I could just become a bum."

Allison gave him a shove and he rolled off her bed and onto the floor, with a thud. "Hey, what was that for?"

"There's no room in my life for someone full of self-pity," Allison said, looking down at him from her bed.

Gary got up and sat on the edge of her bed. Allison sat against the bedboard with her knees pulled up against her chest. He knew she was right. He was just feeling sorry for himself. The problem was, there didn't seem to be anything else to feel.

"I swear, Allison," he said. "For the first time in my life, I really don't know. I used to believe that if you worked hard and kept at it, you'd make it. But now I just don't know."

Gary felt Allison's hands on his shoulders and then her arms came around him from behind and held him tightly. He wished time would stop and he could just stay there forever.

Twenty-five

Gary didn't get home until after dinnertime. He let himself in and walked down the hall past the dining room expecting dinner to be over and the room to be empty. Instead he found his mother, Karl, and Susan sitting around the table having coffee.

"What happened to you tonight?" his mother asked.

"I got delayed," Gary said.

"You know you're supposed to call if you can't make it for dinner," Mrs. Specter said.

Gary shrugged. "Sorry, I forgot. What're you guys doing?"

"We've been talking about last night," Susan said.

"What's there to talk about?" Gary asked.

His mother answered him. "I thought that perhaps, after an experience like that, Susan and Karl might be more receptive to understanding the enormous obstacles that stand before anyone who wants to become a successful musician."

Gary half smiled. His mother sure didn't waste any time. "I'm surprised you didn't just bring out the college applications and have them sign on the dotted line," he said.

His mother frowned. "That's not fair, Gary. We were simply discussing the fact that we are living in a time when the economy is uncertain. People are simply not spending money the way they used to on frivolous things like records. As a result, record companies can't afford to gamble on unproven performers."

"Records aren't frivolous," Gary said. "And a record company isn't gambling. They're paying a group to produce an album. Then the album is sold and the company makes money."

"But the chances of getting a contract are impossible," his mother insisted. "What makes you think that a record company could afford to give hundreds of thousands of dollars away with no assurances that your album would sell? Especially an album by such young and inexperienced musicians as yourselves." Mrs. Specter's voice began to get high and Gary could see that she was getting herself all worked up. "Don't you understand that if you continue in music you're only going to go through more of what you went through last night? People will take advantage of you, they'll lead you down dead-end paths, they'll set you up for all sorts of disappointments."

Gary looked at Susan and Karl and wondered how much of this they believed. No one said a word.

"Well, that's all I have to say," Mrs. Specter said, standing and picking up some empty plates. "I know what you're thinking. You like to cast me in the role of the big, bad meany. Always worrying, always nagging. But it's only for your sake. You're all so young, you have so many opportunities before you. To think that you may be making such a crucial mistake at this time in your life. It's heartbreaking, it really is. Perhaps someday you'll look back and be glad someone in this family was concerned about you. I just hope when that day comes that it won't be too late."

She turned and carried the dishes into the kitchen. Susan and Karl looked up from the table at Gary.

"How long has she been at it?" Gary asked.

"Not very long," Susan said.

"There's nothing like getting hit when you're down, is there," Gary said.

"Maybe some of the things she said make sense," Karl said.

Gary could feel himself grow angry. He wasn't angry at Karl, or at his mother. He was angry because maybe she was right.

Later that night Gary and Karl sat on the floor in Gary's room. Scattered around them were Gary's guitars and amps, his stereo and record collection, and various odds and ends like mike stands, old tape recorders, and a life-size cardboard cutout of Eric Clapton that he'd found behind a record store. Ancient relics, Gary thought bitterly.

A few feet away Karl was in his usual position near the air conditioner, smoking a cigarette and blowing the smoke out the vent. He coughed hoarsely. Gary had never seen him smoke as much as he had since he'd left home. He was really starting to look sickly, his fingers were all yellow with nicotine stains and he had that lousy cough. Now he looked up at Gary.

"Feel like writing a song?"

Gary shook his head.

"Come on, I got a good hook," Karl said. He started tapping out a beat with his hands.

Gary shook his head. "I can't believe you're thinking about writing a song at a time like this."

"Why not?" Karl asked. "What else are we gonna do all night?"

Gary shrugged. Maybe Karl had a point.

"Listen," Karl said, tapping his hands again:

> *"He goes to school and sits in classes all day.*
> *Don't raise his hand, he got nothin' to say.*
> *He wants to split, but the time ain't right.*
> *Oh what a drag, no relief in sight."*

As bummed out as Gary was, he had to admit that it didn't sound too bad. He picked up a pad of paper and started scratching out some more lyrics.

After a few minutes he looked up. "How about this?"

> *"Got to get out, got to get away.*
> *Don't need these hassles every day.*
> *Must be a place where a kid has rights.*
> *Oh what a drag, no relief in sight."*

Karl nodded. Over the next few hours they worked out the rest of the song:

> *"He can't stay home 'cause his parents fight*
> *Eats in McDonald's every night.*
> *He'd like to move out, but he ain't got the might.*
> *Oh what a drag, no relief in sight.*
>
> *"Got to get out, got to move away.*
> *There must be a place where a kid can stay.*
> *He'd pay the money if the price was right.*
> *Oh what a drag, no relief in sight.*
>
> *"His girlfriend works after school.*
> *But he can't hang out 'cause the boss ain't cool.*
> *And her folks won't let her out at night.*
> *Oh what a drag, no relief in sight.*

"Got to get out, got to hide away.
They need a place where they can play.
They want the stars but they don't need the light.
Oh what a drag, no relief in sight.

"He's too young to drive but he's too old to bike,
And cops say, 'Son, you can't hitchhike.'
He can't turn left and he can't turn right.
Oh what a drag, no relief in sight.

"Got to get out, got to ride away.
He'll go anywhere in the U.S. of A.
Just say the word, he's ready to go tonight.
Oh what a drag, no relief in sight."

They finished the song around midnight and Karl went to sleep. But Gary stayed up, sitting on his bed in the dark. Across the room he could see Karl's silhouette as he lay on the mattress he'd been using for a bed. Gary looked down at the pieces of paper they'd written the song on. They were barely visible in his hands. Why, he wondered, had they written it? Did they still believe that they'd have an opportunity to record it someday?

His eyes moved to the black shapes of the four-track tape recorder and mixing board. Had he been kidding himself when he bought that stuff?

Had he been kidding himself about making it in rock and roll? Sure, he always knew it would be tough. Sure, he always knew that most aspiring rock musicians never made it. But he always told himself that he'd be the exception. That he'd be the one in ten thousand who did make it. He never really believed he'd fail, did he? No. He always listened when they said it was nearly impossible to make it, but he never really believed that they'd been talking about him.

Twenty-six

On Thanksgiving Day, Gary sat alone in his room, looking out the window. Across the street, he could see the empty playground. No one was playing there. It was too cold and everyone was getting ready for turkey dinner. The wind blew old brown leaves around the asphalt basketball court and the torn basketball nets fluttered. On a bench next to the fence a solitary figure sat hunched over, his back toward Gary. It was Karl.

Gary knew he wanted to be alone. They all wanted to be alone these days. No one talked about the band much. It seemed like they had reached a dead end. There were no more gigs in small clubs left to play and he doubted that Oscar would have played in them anyway. They had no manager anymore. Gary was certain none of them wanted to hear from or see Barney Star again for as long as they lived.

Across the street in the playground Karl stood up. He

wiped his nose on the sleeve of his jacket, and then started walking slowly back toward the building. Gary felt really bad for him. More than any of them, Karl had believed in Barney Star. In a way, he had to, because if Barney Star failed them, he'd have to go back and face his mother and a lifetime of I-told-you-sos. And now Barney Star had failed them.

A few moments later Gary heard footsteps in the hall. His bedroom door opened slowly and Karl stepped in. He looked at Gary with reddened eyes.

"I guess it's time to go home," he said. "Can't let my old lady eat her frozen TV turkey dinner alone." He started to pick up some of his clothes. "I really appreciate you and your folks letting me stay here all this time."

"It was nothing, Karl," Gary said.

"You know what kills me?" Karl said. "Star must have conned us from the first day. I mean, you know what he was doing in the reception room at Multigram the day we met him? He was just waiting for a couple of naïve guys like us."

"Maybe Star did con us," Gary said. "But I think he got conned too. By the whole show biz dream. It's kind of funny when you think about it. It's like we deserved each other. The dress salesman who thought he could be a hotshot manager and the high school band who thought they could be stars."

"You think it's true, Gary?" Karl asked. "About how impossible it is to make it in music? I mean, when you start thinking about it, it really seems kind of crazy. Even if you get a record contract it doesn't mean anything. Look at the Zoomies."

"I know," Gary said.

"And you know what I noticed?" Karl said. "You look on TV and see those rock videos. Every month it seems like there are twenty new groups. But a year later, nineteen of them have completely disappeared."

Gary nodded. In the old days he would have argued that they would be the one band in twenty that would still be around after a year. But now his heart just wasn't in it.

Twenty-seven

It was exam time at Lenox Prep and Karl and Oscar were suddenly busy studying. Susan was writing away for college catalogs and talking about taking her SATs over again. Working full time in the ice cream shop had convinced her that if the band wasn't going anywhere, there might be some advantages to higher education.

Gary still didn't know what to do. The others were pursuing alternatives, making preparations just in case the band was unable to get going again. But he couldn't figure out what his alternatives were. It had been "The band or nothing" for so long. Maybe, like Johnny Fantasy, he could do session work, signing on as a hired musician to play other people's music. Maybe he could do advertising jingles or weddings. It sounded slightly less than thrilling, but what if he didn't have a choice?

In the meantime, if anyone asked what his plans were, he decided to tell them he was in training to become a school-crossing guard. He sure was spending enough time standing around in front of Allison's school to qualify.

After walking her to ballet class one freezing-cold day, Gary turned toward home. It was so cold that he was almost jogging by the time he reached the block where the empty lots were. As he passed one of the lots, he heard noises coming from behind a tall mound of refuse. It sounded like a scuffle or a fight. Gary could hear taunts and threats. One of the voices sounded like Thomas's.

Gary quickly turned off the sidewalk and cut across the lot. "Come on, tough guy," someone was saying. "Let's see how tough you really are." The sound of a struggle followed. Gary came around the mound of garbage just in time to see three kids roughing up a smaller kid. In the freezing afternoon air they were trying to pull the smaller kid's leather jacket off. The smaller kid was trying to fight back, but he was obviously overpowered. Gary realized it was Thomas. Somehow he'd always known that Thomas would get himself into a mess like that.

"Hey, lay off!" Gary screamed at the kids. He picked up a long piece of rusty pipe from the pile of refuse.

The three kids suddenly stopped. By now they'd gotten Thomas's jacket off.

"Get away from him!" Gary shouted, moving closer with the pipe. The last thing in the world he wanted to do was use it. But if it came to protecting his little brother, he knew he would.

The kids let go, and Thomas quickly ran toward Gary. He could see that his little brother was crying. Meanwhile, the others turned and ran out of the lot with Thomas's leather jacket. They were laughing.

Gary dropped the pipe. Thomas was standing in his shirt sleeves with his back toward him, sniffing and wiping the tears from his eyes, refusing to let his brother see his face. Gary took off his own jacket and put it around Thomas's shoulders. "Come on, killer," he said, "let's go home."

At their house, Gary went in first to make sure the coast was clear. Thomas's face was scratched. His jeans were torn and dirty. He didn't want their parents to see him like that. Gary came back to the door and told him to go upstairs to the bathroom and wash up. Then he went to his brother's room and got him some fresh clothes.

Gary had not been in his brother's room in a long time. Things had definitely changed. The old plastic models of army tanks and fighter planes were gone and now Thomas had posters of rock bands up on his walls. The bands in Thomas's posters were those loud heavy-metal groups who always dressed in black leather jackets and silver studs and heavy boots. Gary chuckled.

He heard the door open and Thomas slipped in wearing a towel around his waist and carrying his dirty clothes under his arm.

"What're you looking at?" he asked.

"Your posters," Gary said. He noticed that his brother's face was pretty scratched up. "You figure out yet what you're gonna tell Mom and Dad when they ask you how you got those scratches?" he asked.

"I don't know," Thomas said as he pulled on a fresh pair of jeans.

"You could tell them you were climbing a tree in the park and slipped and the branches hit your face," Gary suggested.

"Kids climb trees," Thomas said.

"Believe it or not, they still think you're a kid," Gary said.

Thomas shrugged. Gary knew he probably wanted to be left alone. He headed for the door.

"Hey, Gary?" Thomas said.

Gary stopped. "Yeah?"

"You won't tell anyone how it really happened, will you?"

"No, of course not."

Thomas smiled a little. "Thanks."

Gary went downstairs to make some hot chocolate. His mother was in the kitchen.

"Oh, Gary, you got some calls today," she said.

"From who?" he asked.

"I took the names and numbers and left them by the phone."

Gary scowled and quickly went to the phone. He wasn't expecting a call from anyone except Allison. He picked up the list of messages. The first was from Boudini Caterers, the second from the Lewd, the third from Fortunado Florists. All the messages were the same. Please call as soon as possible.

Gary dialed the number of the florist. A female voice answered and Gary explained who he was. The female voice told him to hold on. Soon a deep and husky male voice got on the phone.

"Gary Specter?"

"Yes?"

"Are you familiar with a catering job we did a few weeks ago at a club called the Lewd? It looks like it was a party or something."

"Yeah, it was a showcase," Gary said.

"Well, we got a bill here for four hundred fifty-eight dollars worth of flowers. Would you mind paying it?"

"But our manager was supposed to take care of that," Gary said.

"You talking about some character named Barney Star?" the husky voice said.

"Uh, yes."

"He originally paid for the bill on a credit card," the voice said. "Turns out the card was no good. If you know where that guy is, the credit card company would appreciate you telling them."

"How'd you get my name and number?" Gary asked.

"It's written right here on the bill," the voice said. "Your buddy Mr. Star must have written it down."

"But why do I have to pay the bill?" Gary asked.

"Your manager, your party, your flowers."

"But he's not our manager anymore," Gary said. "He never really was."

"Listen, kid," the husky voice said, getting tough. "I don't really care who pays that bill as long as it gets paid, understand? Makes no difference to me whether it's paid by you, your manager, or your long-lost uncle in Alaska. The only difference is, I don't have a phone number for your manager or your long-lost uncle. But I do have one for you. Get the point?"

Gary got the point. Either he paid the bill or who knew what the guy would do.

After he hung up, he called the caterer and the Lewd. The story was the same. The bills were unpaid, there was no trace of Mr. Star, and Gary's name and number were left on the bill.

Barney Star had not only failed miserably, he'd left a legacy: nearly three thousand dollars in unpaid bills.

Gary put the phone down. For the first time in days he felt something besides hopeless depression. Specifically, he felt like committing murder and mayhem upon the body of Barney Star. How could the guy do something like that and not tell them? *Why* would he do something like that?

Gary couldn't believe it. He had to talk to the other band members. He called Karl.

"How are things with your mom?" he asked.

"Aw, not so bad. We've had a couple of long talks about what happened and she's not so angry anymore. But it's still a kind of touchy subject."

"You tell her what happened at the showcase?" Gary asked.

"Yeah. I think that secretly she was kind of pleased that we learned our lesson."

Just wait, Gary thought. Then he said, "Listen, you still have that business card Star gave you? The one with his phone number on it?"

"Yeah, but forget it, Gary," the drummer said.

"What do you mean?"

"Well, I decided to call him a couple of days ago," Karl said. "I guess I just wanted to ask if he knew why no one showed up at the showcase. But anyway, his phone's been disconnected."

"Why didn't you tell me?" Gary asked.

"I figured it didn't matter," Karl said. "I mean, I didn't think we were going to keep him as our manager anyway. So what did you want the number for?"

Gary told him about the unpaid bills.

"Oh-oh," Karl said. "Sounds like we are in deep trouble."

"Do me a favor," Gary said. "Call Oscar and tell him we have to meet at the ice cream shop tomorrow after school. Okay?"

"Aye-aye, captain."

Twenty-eight

For the first time in weeks, Gary felt a sense of purpose, even if that purpose was only to find some way around paying Barney Star's debt. After dinner that night, Gary put on his leather jacket and went back out into the frigid cold. His destination was Allison's apartment building.

The doorman wouldn't let him go up without first buzzing Allison's apartment. When he got off the elevator on her floor, she was waiting in the foyer.

"What is it, Gary?"

He told her about the unpaid bills.

"Well, my grandmother used to say that when it rains, it pours," Allison said, pulling him by the hand.

"Where are we going?" he asked.

"Into the den to see my father."

Gary hesitated.

"Oh, come on, he's not going to bite you." Allison tugged at his hand.

Gary allowed himself to be led down the hall and into the room where Mr. Ollquist sat at a desk reading some papers and making notes on a yellow legal pad. The walls of the room were covered with bookcases filled with books, but on one shelf there was a color television set showing a football game with the sound off. Mr. Ollquist was wearing a tie, but it was loosened at the neck and his jacket was hanging over the back of the chair. His shirt sleeves were rolled up.

"Dad?" Allison said.

Mr. Ollquist looked up. "Well, hello, Gary." He stood up and subjected Gary's hand to a bone cruncher. Gary knew that if he was going to continue to see Allison, he was going to have to find some way of avoiding those handshakes.

"Can you help Gary with a legal question?" Allison asked her father.

Mr. Ollquist looked surprised, but said, "Of course. I'm not sure I'll know the answer, but sit down." He gestured to two chairs on the side of the room. Gary brought them closer to the desk and he and Allison sat.

It took Gary a couple of minutes to tell the whole story. When he finished he said, "Basically, what we need to know is, are we responsible for those bills?"

Mr. Ollquist pursed his lips together and tapped the pencil against the pad of paper. "You say you agreed to let this Star fellow represent you and that your band used all the services that you were billed for?"

"More or less," Gary said.

Mr. Ollquist nodded slowly. "I'm afraid you probably are responsible. You could let them take you to court, but to be frank, it would cost you more to hire a lawyer to represent you than it would to just pay the bills."

"Isn't there anything Gary can do?" Allison asked.

"Well, your one hope is to find this Barney Star," Mr. Ollquist said. "But from what you've told me, I doubt Mr. Star wants to be found."

Gary and Allison glanced at each other. Gary shrugged.

"If you'd like, Gary," Allison's father said, "I could talk to these people. If nothing else, we could set up a schedule for repayment so they don't all come hounding you at once."

"Thanks, Mr. Ollquist," Gary said. "I guess I'll have to talk it over with the rest of the band and let you know. You've been a real help."

There didn't seem to be any more to say, so Gary and Allison started to get up. But then Mr. Ollquist cleared his throat.

"Tell me, is this going to be a severe blow to your music career?"

"To tell you the truth, Mr. Ollquist, the band is pretty badly bummed out," Gary said.

"You're not going to let this one incident take the wind out of your sails, are you?" Allison's father asked.

"Well, it's not just this incident," Gary said. "It's a lot of incidents and a lot of frustration and a lot of banging our heads against the wall and not getting anywhere."

Mr. Ollquist made a fist. "Remember, Gary. Persevere." Then he winked.

Gary smiled. The guy wasn't so bad after all.

Gary persevered straight through until the following afternoon when he met the band at the ice cream shop. It was another freezing-cold day and business at the shop was anything but brisk. The band sat around one of the marble tables. For once, no one wanted any free ice cream. After Gary told them about the bills they didn't have much of an appetite.

"We don't have to pay," Oscar insisted. "Barney Star arranged that showcase. They should go find him."

Gary glanced at the others around the table. They'd been there so often lately that Susan had put a little "Reserved" sign on it.

"They'll never find him," he said. "This afternoon I went to see Murray Weinburger, that old guy who made our costumes, remember? Those costumes cost eight hundred bucks and Barney stiffed him too."

"Does he want us to pay?" Susan asked.

Gary shook his head. "He's all right. He said he didn't want to make it any harder on us than it already was. But he also said that deep down Barney was okay."

"Oh, sure," Oscar laughed.

"No, I can believe it now," Gary told him. "Barney really tried. He just didn't know what he was doing. Murray told me that a couple of bands really took him for a ride, getting him to buy them expensive equipment and instruments and then not showing up for gigs and stuff. Barney went broke. We were his last chance. He figured if he could get us a record contract, he could pay the bills off with his share of the advance. It was a gamble, and it just didn't work."

"So all those stories about his other bands getting signed for three-album contracts, and the press conferences and secret recording sessions—that was all bull," Karl said.

"He was trying to get us to believe in him," Gary said.

"I wish he'd just told us the truth," Susan said.

"He couldn't," Gary said. "We never would have let him work for us. I'm not saying that lying to us was right. But I can understand why he did it. It was just his dream. The whole music business is built on dreams. It's just that most of them don't come true."

"Only the nightmares like this come true," Karl said. "I mean, how are we gonna come up with three thousand bucks?"

"We don't have to come up with a penny," Oscar insisted.

"We do, Oscar," Gary said. "I talked to Allison's father last night and we're legally obligated to do it."

"I don't feel legally obligated to do anything," Oscar

snapped. "Especially pay for a showcase that turned out to be a complete joke."

Gary stared at the keyboard player, feeling his anger growing. "Oscar, can't you see that things are bad enough and we don't need you making them worse?" he said. "Why do you always have to be so disagreeable?"

"Because it's not my problem," Oscar snapped. "I'm a musician, not a lawyer."

"Well, I'll tell you, Oscar," Gary said. "If we don't pay those bills it's gonna hurt the band's reputation. You know, these club owners all talk to each other. If word gets around that we stiffed the Lewd, it's going to be impossible for us to get gigs anywhere else."

"I thought we were finished doing gigs in those clubs," Oscar said.

"Well, I can't think of any other way to make back the money we owe," Gary said.

Oscar stood up. "Forget it. I'm not going back to those clubs anymore. I don't care who we owe money to. It's not my problem." He started to put his coat on. "Frankly, I have no intention of paying anyone anything."

He started to walk toward the door. Karl began to say something, but Gary stopped him. He was so mad at Oscar that he was ready to let him quit.

When no one begged him to stop, Oscar stopped near the door and looked back at them. "You'll just have to go find yourself another keyboard player," he said. "I don't care."

He took another step toward the door and then looked back at them again. "That's right, I'm quitting the band. You hear? Quitting."

When no one answered, he took a few steps more and then turned yet again. "You'll have to go find another composer too," he said.

Gary could feel Susan and Karl glancing nervously at him. Wasn't he going to beg Oscar to stay, just like all the times in the past? No, he was sick and tired of it. Instead he said the first thing that came into his mind. "I already did."

Oscar and the other members of the band gaped at him.

"I knew this would happen," Gary said. "So yesterday I went to see Charlie. You remember that kid who was always bugging us at our gigs? Well, he really wants to join the band. And he's not a bad keyboard player, either." Gary glanced at Karl. "Right, Karl?"

"Uh, yeah," Karl said, nodding. "He's a pretty damn good keyboard player."

"And he's got some good songs too," Gary added.

Oscar gave them a look of incredible fury and then grabbed the door, went out, and slammed it behind him.

Silence descended on the ice cream shop. The loudest noise was a faucet dripping behind the counter. Susan and Karl turned and looked at Gary.

"I'm sorry," he said quietly. "I just couldn't take any more of his threats and temper tantrums."

"But Charlie doesn't even play keyboard," Karl said. "He's a guitar player."

"I know," Gary said. "I'm sorry, really. It wasn't a well-thought-out thing. Someone just had to tell Oscar that even as good as he is, he's not God's gift to rock and roll."

"Well, I'm glad you did it," Susan said. "It's about time someone put him in his place."

"But now how are we going to play?" Karl asked.

"We'll manage somehow. Maybe we'll get another keyboard player somewhere," Gary said. "There are always guys looking to hook up with a band. You see ads in the back of the *Voice* all the time."

"The baby-sitters will never forgive us," Karl said.

"I don't know," Gary said. "I'm sure you could do that song just as well as Oscar."

Karl shook his head. "Forget it. There's no way I'm going out sucking my thumb and dragging that stupid pacifier."

Susan nudged Gary. "Now he's starting to act like Oscar."

Gary leaned back and tilted his chair legs up. He couldn't explain why, but suddenly he felt relieved, as if a big burden had been lifted off his shoulders.

"You know what?" he said. "I know we need an album contract and we need to become a bigger, more popular group. But we don't have to do it this month, or even this year. And we don't have to leave all the little clubs, either. Those clubs are where we started. They're where our first fans saw us. And I still love playing in those places. I like being close to the audience and knowing half of them by name. I think it's really wrong of us to suddenly decide we're just too good to play in those places anymore. They gave us our start. And if we ever go anywhere in this business, we'll owe a lot of it to them."

He looked at Karl and Susan. "I think half the reason we've been so depressed lately is because we just haven't been playing. And that's another reason for going back to those clubs. We'll still be trying for that record contract and a shot at DeLux and the big time. But in the meantime we'll keep gigging. You with me?"

Karl and Susan nodded.

"But what about the money?" Karl asked.

"Allison's father says he'll set up some kind of repayment schedule. Maybe we'll have to pay back twenty bucks a week or something. In the meantime, I'll arrange all our gigs and we'll get someone to drive the van for us."

Gary paused and studied their faces. "Listen," he said. "I know we've just been through a really bad experience, but at least we've learned something from it. We'll know next time to find out a lot more about a manager before we even agree to let him or her do anything for us. And if we ever have another showcase, we'll make sure we know who's paying for it first. I mean, that's simple stuff. The important thing is, will you try again? Will you do it?"

"I'll do it," Karl said. "I never understood what was so bad about playing those small clubs in the first place."

"Me too," Susan said. "If I have to sell ice cream all week, at least I might as well have some fun on the weekends."

Just then the front door of the shop swung open and Oscar stormed back in, his coat and shirt tails flying.

"How dare you!" he screamed at Gary. "How dare you threaten to replace me. How dare you think that I'd just walk away from this band. This band is as much mine as it is any of yours. You can't replace me. I won't let you. I don't care if we play gigs in the men's room at Grand Central Terminal. I will not leave this band and you can't make me."

With that, Oscar sat down at the table and crossed his arms.

Gary glanced at the other members of the table. "Well, Oscar, if you insist."

"I absolutely insist," he snapped. "The nerve of you, trying to replace me."

"We're going to have to go back to playing in the dumps for a while," Susan told him.

"I'll suffer," Oscar said.

"We're gonna have to pay the Lewd and the others back," Karl said.

"Don't try to frighten me away," Oscar said resolutely. "Because I won't go. It's as simple as that."

"What do you think?" Gary asked Karl and Susan.

But before they could answer, Oscar said, "Cut the act, Gary. We all know Charlie doesn't even play the keyboard."

Gary just grinned.

Twenty-nine

The band went back to work. Acting as their manager, Gary booked them into the clubs, arranged dates, and haggled over how much the band would be paid and how long their sets would be. Pretty soon they were playing the same old clubs, and Gary was working twice as hard as ever. But he couldn't have been happier. Getting ahead and making it was important, but Gary knew he'd never forget that the reason he was a rock-and-roll musician wasn't that he wanted to make a million dollars or see himself on a TV rock video. The reason he was a musician was that he loved playing the music. It was in his blood.

Everything went back to normal. Including his mother.

Clunk! Clunk! Clunk! "Gary!"

Clunk! Clunk! Clunk! "Telephone!"

She couldn't stop him from playing rock and roll. She couldn't make him go to college. But she could always wake him up.

Gary entered the kitchen yawning and stretching. "Know

who it is?" he asked his mother, who was sitting at the counter having her morning fix of caffeine.

"Someone named Rick Jones," his mother said.

Gary suddenly felt wide awake. Rick Jones? The A and R man from Multigram? What in the world could he want? Gary quickly picked up the phone. "Hello?"

"Gary? Listen, this is Rick Jones over at Multigram," the A and R man said. "I finally had a chance to listen to your demo record yesterday and you know, it's pretty good."

"It is?" Gary said. Actually, he always knew it was. He just couldn't believe Rick Jones thought so too.

"Now listen, Gary," Jones said. "The opening act at DeLux canceled for tonight and we've been talking to the management over there about having one of our new prospects fill in. Do you think your band could make it?"

"You mean play? Tonight? At DeLux?"

"Can you do it?" Jones asked.

"But I don't understand," Gary gasped. "I mean . . ."

"Look, don't worry about understanding," Jones said. "Just worry about getting your band down to DeLux. Okay? You've got three hours."

"Uh . . ."

"Seven o'clock for a sound check."

When he hung up the phone, his mother asked him what that was all about. But Gary was too dazed to respond.

"Gary, what's wrong?" Mrs. Specter asked.

"Wrong?" Gary asked, still in shock.

"Who is Rick Jones?" his mother said.

Gary began to come to his senses. He had to get hold of the band members fast. He picked up the phone.

"Gary, you haven't answered my question," his mother said.

"Rick Jones is an A and R guy at Multigram Records," Gary said as he quickly dialed Susan's number at the ice cream shop. "They want to hear us play at DeLux tonight. It's a really important club—the big time, Mom."

His mother nodded weakly, and looked upward toward the ceiling. "I have tried," she said. "I have done everything within my power. It's hopeless."

The next few hours were a total panic. Oscar and Karl rushed to Gary's. Susan told her boss there had been a sudden injury in the family. Everyone was doing three things at once to prepare for the gig.

They didn't have time to stop and wonder how it came about or what it meant. They were too busy looking for mike cords and fuzz pedals and a million other things. Karl persuaded his mother to rent a van and help them get over to the club. Mrs. Roesch was understandably unenthusiastic, but Karl convinced her that this was a matter of life and death.

A short while later she pulled up in front of Gary's house with the van. As they were bringing the amps and guitars down the front steps, Thomas arrived home from school.

"Hey, what's going on?" he asked.

"We got a sound check at DeLux at seven,'" Gary said as he picked up an amp and put it into the van.

"Oh," Thomas said. He looked into the back of the van where Susan was trying to arrange all the equipment. "You're never gonna get it all in that way."

"Want to show me how?" Susan asked.

Thomas glanced at Gary. "Sure," he said, dropping his books and jumping up into the van. With his help they broke their previous records for van packing and were quickly off to Oscar's.

Thomas had Oscar's ironing board and synthesizer packed in a flash and soon they were all squeezed in the van and bouncing downtown as fast as Mrs. Roesch could go. Gary and Oscar were crouched over a piece of paper, trying to figure out the set list of songs they wanted to play. Susan was replacing one of the strings on her bass and Karl was trying to fix a broken foot pedal. Everyone was nervous and excited and scared. It was just like old times.

At DeLux, Mrs. Roesch parked the van in the back by the stage door. But before they could even start to unload, two stagehands ran out of the back entrance.

"The Coming Attractions?" one of them asked.

"Yes," Karl said.

"Go ahead in," the stagehand said, pointing toward the door. "They're waiting inside."

"What about the equipment?" Thomas asked.

"Don't worry," the stagehand said. "We'll take care of it."

The band stared at each other in disbelief. They couldn't believe the special treatment. They waited for just a moment while Oscar gave the stagehands special instructions for the handling of his ironing board, and then hurried inside.

It was a huge, cavernous club, far bigger than anything the band had ever played in. In the backstage area dozens of people—roadies, sound men, musicians, and groupies—were rushing around, getting ready for the night's triple bill, which now included Gary Specter and the Coming Attractions Plus Oscar. The band looked on in wonderment. Not only was the place huge, but they'd never seen so much lighting and sound equipment.

A neatly dressed man with short brown hair came toward them. He was wearing jeans and a blue crew-neck sweater and carried a clipboard. He seemed to be the only calm person in the whole place.

"You must be the Coming Attractions," he said with a friendly smile. "I'm Jim Stone, manager of DeLux. We're glad you could make it."

"So are we," Karl said.

Stone turned to Karl's mother and shook her hand. "You must be Mrs. Roesch."

"Yes," Mrs. Roesch said.

"Well, I'm sorry about the short notice," Stone said. "But we've heard such great things about your band that when we got a cancellation for tonight's show we naturally wanted to get you."

Mrs. Roesch forced a smile on her face. "Naturally," she said.

"Why don't you and I go back to my office and work out the terms for tonight's performance," Jim Stone said. He turned to the rest of the band. "In the meantime, take care of your sound check and get ready for your set. If you need anything, just give a yell."

Gary nodded, but he was nervous about Mrs. Roesch. After she and Stone left for the office, he turned to Karl.

"What's the story with your mom?" he asked.

"I don't know," Karl said. "I guess she's gonna play manager for the night."

"Is she still mad?" Thomas asked.

"Wouldn't you be?" Karl asked.

"I wish there was something we could do," Susan said.

Just then, Rick Jones appeared, wearing a shiny red baseball jacket, tight blue jeans, and cowboy boots.

"Hey, guys, I'm glad you could make it." He shook Gary's hand and turned to the rest of the band. "Listen, I'm Rick Jones and I've heard your demo and I think it's real good stuff."

Nobody knew what to say. Jones's interest was a dramatic change from the way he'd treated Gary and Karl when they went to his office.

"Now, look, I want to show you something," Jones said. He led them over to the side of the stage where they could peak out from the curtain. DeLux had a big flat dance floor where most of the crowd would gather later. But there were also balconies that rose on either side of the floor and there the band could see tables being prepared.

Rick Jones pointed up to the second balcony. "Now I'm going to be sitting up there tonight at a private table with a couple of heavies from Multigram. They don't know who you are yet so your job is to make them interested in you. The more interested, the better. Understand?"

The band nodded.

"Good," Jones said. "Now you just get your act together and put on the best damn show you can, okay? And when you're done, make sure you and your manager come up to the second balcony and have a drink. We'll be expecting you, right?"

The band nodded again. Gary knew the others must have been wondering, what manager?

Rick Jones smiled. "Okay, guys, good luck." He started to walk away, but Gary and Karl followed him.

"Excuse me, Mr. Jones?" Gary said.

Jones stopped and they caught up to him near the side of the stage. They were far enough away so the rest of the band couldn't hear them over the noise and bustling backstage.

"I don't get it," Gary said. "It's been months since we came to your office."

"And you weren't exactly thrilled when we were there," Karl added.

Jones just shrugged. "Listen, guys, I see so many bands a week, how could I know? When the word came down from upstairs, and I mean, *way upstairs*, I dug out your single and it was good. I just don't understand why you didn't tell me in the first place."

"Tell you what?" Gary asked.

"Who you knew," Jones said, looking around impatiently. "Look, I've got to run. If you put on a show that's as decent as that single, you'll be in good shape, okay? See you later." He walked away quickly.

Meanwhile, Karl looked at Gary. "What did he mean by that? The word came down from way upstairs?"

Gary shrugged. "You got me, Karl. Maybe the magic rock-and-roll fairy works for Multigram."

Later that night the band took their positions behind their instruments and mikes. When the curtain opened it was a truly awe-inspiring moment and only slightly less than terrifying. They had never stood before such a huge crowd. Hundreds and hundreds—maybe even a thousand people filled the giant dance floor and lined the walls. While Jim Stone introduced the band, Gary and the other members looked at each other in disbelief.

"Now I know what the big in big time means," Karl mumbled nervously, from the drum set.

Gary nodded. "There's only one thing we can do, guys," he whispered, looking from Karl to Susan to Oscar. "Just play."

Jim Stone stepped off the stage, the house lights went down, and half a dozen spotlights flashed on, glaring straight down into the band's eyes. A loud murmur rushed through the crowd when they realized that Gary was wearing a straitjacket. But already he was counting down to the opening notes of their old standard, "Rock Therapy."

> *"I need Rock, Rock, Rock Therapy,*
> *I need Rock, Rock, Rock Therapy.*
> *Don't you hook up no electrodes to me.*
> *I need Rock, Rock, Rock Therapy."*

The band played hard and tight. Up on the stage Gary really shook it, dancing and strutting up and down as far as his guitar cord would let him go. He felt like he was sweating twice as much as normal—half from the heat of the stage and half from plain old nerves.

As they played, Gary was really glad to see them working together again. But it wasn't like the old days, when they were a bunch of naïve kids with stars in their eyes. They'd learned some tough lessons, some things they weren't going to forget. As the band paused between songs, he gazed up into the big dark club, wondering what Rick Jones and the honchos from Multigram were thinking. He wanted them to know that he really appreciated them giving him and his band an opportunity to play. But he also wanted them to know that they'd seen the other side of the rock-and-roll business and it wasn't something they were going to forget.

Gary leaned toward the microphone. "This next song," he told the crowd, "is for everyone who ever tried to make it in rock and roll." Behind him Oscar whipped up an instrumental introduction. The band joined in as Gary sang:

> "You call the man, but he don't call back
> 'Cause your demo's just gotten lost in the stack.
> You're so mad that you could lose control.
> Well, them's the breaks in rock and roll."

The rest of the band sang the chorus:

> "Well, them's the breaks in rock and roll.
> Yeah, them's the breaks in rock and roll.
> You say the business ain't got no soul?
> Well, them's the breaks in rock and roll."

Oscar took a verse:

> "You knock on doors till your knuckles are raw.
> You beg and beg till you get lockjaw.
> You can threaten, you can scream and cajole.
> But they won't hear you in rock and roll."

Then Susan belted the next:

> *"You got your music, but nothin' to eat.*
> *You're so desperate that you play on the street.*
> *You catch pneumonia 'cause you live in a hole.*
> *But there's no welfare in rock and roll."*

They went into the break. As Gary ripped leads off the Stratocaster, he had one eye on the audience watching for their reactions. Maybe they hadn't expected much, but the band was determined to make sure they never forgot them.

It was Karl's turn:

> *"You spend your life trying to beat the clock.*
> *You got one wish—that's to make it in rock.*
> *You love the music, but it takes its toll.*
> *Nothing comes easy in rock and roll."*

And Gary sang the last verse:

> *"For twenty years you've made the rounds.*
> *And every day you've been shot down.*
> *Maybe twenty more before you reach your goal.*
> *But that's life in rock and roll."*

Finally the band sang together:

> *"It's tough, it's rough in rock and roll.*
> *They'll beat you and mistreat you in rock and roll,*
> *'Cause it's the business that's got no soul*
> *It's just the breaks in rock and roll."*

It seemed like almost no time had passed and suddenly Oscar was on his knees at the front of the stage, the microphone clasped in his hands before him, wailing about his eternal love for his baby-sitter.

Gary couldn't believe the set had gone that quickly. He wanted to stay and play in front of that huge crowd for another two hours at least, but offstage he could see Jim Stone waving and pointing to his wristwatch. Time was up and Gary knew that if they ever wanted to get invited back to DeLux again, they had to get off the stage, and make way for the next group.

When they finally left the stage, the crowd was on its feet, cheering. The band was ecstatic. It had been a great show, maybe one of the best they'd ever given. A crowd of people waited offstage to congratulate them. Thomas had towels for them to dry off with and even Mrs. Roesch looked pleased. For a few minutes they were surrounded by technicians, stagehands, and backstage groupies. Everyone wanted to know who they were and where they'd come from. Then the next group went onstage and the crowd around the Coming Attractions began to dwindle.

The band didn't mind. Finally they were alone. They sat on their amps and guitar cases and drank cold beers and sodas. Karl wiped his forehead with his towel. "Hey, look." He gestured toward the rear stage entrance. The band turned and saw that Mrs. Roesch was standing off to the side by herself, smoking a cigarette, and watching the group that had followed the Coming Attractions onstage.

Gary glanced back at the band. "Are you guys thinking what I'm thinking?" he asked.

Everyone nodded and together they got up and walked over to Mrs. Roesch. Gary was in the lead. As usual they were going to let him do the talking. "Uh, Mrs. Roesch?"

Karl's mother turned. "Yes, Gary?"

Gary twisted his towel nervously in his hands. "Mrs. Roesch, I think we know that we made a mistake and we can understand that you're really mad at us," he said. "I mean, Barney Star really had us seeing all kinds of stars and stuff. I know it's our fault, but he really did a con job."

Mrs. Roesch nodded slowly.

"This may sound dumb," Gary said. "But I think we've learned our lesson."

"You were with us from the beginning," Susan said.

"And you never made any promises you couldn't keep," Karl said.

"So I guess what we're wondering," Gary said, "is if you'd be our manager again."

Mrs. Roesch looked around at the rest of the members of the band. "And the rest of you feel that way?" she asked.

Everyone nodded enthusiastically. Even Oscar.

Karl's mother was quiet for a few seconds. Then she took a deep drag on her cigarette and exhaled. "Well, I really do appreciate that," she said. "But I'm afraid I can't."

"Why not?" Susan asked.

"I'll tell you, Susan," Mrs. Roesch said. "Over the last few weeks I've done a lot of thinking and I've realized something. As angry as I was about what happened, in a way I was also relieved. All of a sudden I didn't have to spend every free moment after work calling clubs and hounding record companies and working on the band's business. You have no idea how exhausting it is to look after all the details, from keeping dates straight to constantly hassling with club managers over money. Not only was it horribly aggravating, but it took up all my spare time. One morning I woke up and said to myself, 'You're lucky you don't have to do that anymore.'"

"But what will we do for a manager?" Karl asked.

"Oh, I don't think you'll have any problem getting yourself a new manager," his mother told him. "And a good one too. Someone who really does know the business. I'll say this for you kids, you've just been through a pretty bad time. I think a lot of bands would have gone through an experience like that and just given up. But you stuck with it. I think that means something. In fact, I think that means a lot. You're going to go a long way and I think you should have someone with a good head for business and a lot of experience."

The band looked at each other. Talk about good news and bad news. . . . Everyone looked a little confused. Gary looked back at Mrs. Roesch. "But we don't want to, uh, just lose you."

"I have no intention of being lost," Mrs. Roesch said. "As far as I'm concerned, I'm still the mother of your drummer. Besides, you're still not old enough to rent a van yourself. So if you like, I'll just continue as your driver."

"Yeah, sure," Karl said. "That would be great, Mom."

"But do you think that you could be our temporary manager until we get a new one?" Gary asked.

Mrs. Roesch sighed. "Do you really feel you need a temporary manager?" she asked.

"Absolutely," Oscar said. "For instance, we need someone to remind us that if we don't get upstairs to those guys on the second balcony pretty soon they're gonna forget about us."

"All right," Mrs. Roesch said. "As your van driver and temporary manager, my first suggestion is that you get your tails up to the second balcony and talk to those gentlemen from Multigram Records before they get impatient."

Up on the second balcony, the Multigram Records table was covered with glasses and bottles and overflowing ashtrays. More than a dozen people—women, men, all very stylishly dressed—were sitting around the table talking loudly and obviously enjoying themselves.

When Gary and the rest of the band got there, Rick Jones stood up. "That was great, really terrific," he said, patting Gary and Oscar on the shoulders. "Come on, I want you to meet our director of new talent development."

Jones led them around the table to a man with shortish hair who was wearing a dark business suit. He certainly didn't fit Gary's idea of a record executive. He looked a lot more like a lawyer.

"This is Hank Finney," Jones told the band. Then, turning to Finney, he said, "Hank, I really think these kids are something. Probably the best discovery I've made since the Frenetic Motormouth Orchestra."

Finney nodded and turned toward the band. "You kids have any contractual obligations to any other record company?" he asked.

"No, they're free and clear," Mrs. Roesch said.

Finney said something else, but Gary didn't hear him. He'd just noticed two girls standing nearby. It couldn't be. Allison and Tina? He glanced at Finney and then back at the girls again. But how?

"We are committed to a program of developing new talent," Finney was saying. Gary kept glancing at the girls. What were they doing here? How could they have found out? He couldn't wait to talk to them. Tina and Allison watched him and giggled.

"What I think we'd like to do," Finney was saying, "is discuss this further. Perhaps next week."

"I'm sure that will be fine with them," Jones said eagerly. "Right?"

The band nodded. It looked like Finney was finished with them, but then Jones started to introduce them to a slightly heavy-set woman holding a wineglass. "Now this is our director of publicity." But Gary slipped away and went over to Allison and Tina.

"What are you guys doing here?" he asked in a low voice.

"We wanted to hear you play," Tina said.

"But how did you know?" Gary asked, looking from Tina to Allison and back. "I mean, we only found out this afternoon."

The two girls looked at each other and giggled.

Suddenly something popped into his mind. "Wait a minute!" he said, looking at Allison. "Your father's friend. The president of Multigram."

"All he did was ask someone to listen to your single," Allison said.

"I can't believe it!" Gary said. "You were behind all this?"

"Isn't she wonderful?" Tina giggled.

"Stop it, Tina," Allison said, but she was smiling. "It wasn't me, it was my father. I actually forgot about his friend at Multigram."

"Unbelievable," Gary muttered.

By now the other members of the band had noticed them.

"Hey, what are you guys doing here?" Karl asked.

"Just hanging around," Tina said with a grin.

"Guys," Gary said. "I think I have discovered the identity of the magic rock-and-roll fairy."

"What's he talking about?" Oscar asked.

"He's about six feet two," Gary said. "Probably weighs a hundred and ninety pounds and is a senior partner at the law firm of Dewey, Cheathem, and Howe."

"Are you feeling all right?" Susan asked.

"He is also the father of this wonder girl," Gary said, embracing Allison.

"Gary, don't." Allison made a feeble attempt to stop him.

"Here comes the mushy part," Karl groaned.

"How cute," Tina said.

"How infantile," Oscar said.

Gary hugged Allison. He didn't care what they thought.

The other members of the band turned away to leave them alone. Somewhere in the background, Gary could hear Rick Jones bragging about the great discovery he'd made. Go ahead and brag, Gary thought. They were on their way again. That was all that mattered.

TODD STRASSER is the author of four highly praised novels: *Workin' for Peanuts, Friends Till the End,* and *Rock 'n' Roll Nights,* published by Delacorte Press and available in Dell Laurel-Leaf editions; his *Angel Dust Blues* is also available in a Dell Laurel-Leaf edition. *Friends Till the End* and *Rock 'n' Roll Nights* were named Young Adult Services Best Books by the American Library Association. *Turn It Up!* is a companion to *Rock 'n' Roll Nights.*

Mr. Strasser's writing has appeared in many publications, including *The New Yorker* and *The New York Times.* He grew up on Long Island and now lives in New York City. He is currently at work on the third book in Gary Specter's story.